D0341617

The Rat Prince

THE Rat Prince

Bridget Hodder

Margaret Ferguson Books
FARRAR STRAUS GIROUX
New York

Farrar Straus Giroux Books for Young Readers
175 Fifth Avenue, New York 10010

Text copyright © 2016 by Bridget Hodder
All rights reserved
Printed in the United States of America by R. R. Donnelley & Sons Company,
Harrisonburg, Virginia
First edition, 2016
1 3 5 7 9 10 8 6 4 2

mackids.com

Library of Congress Cataloging-in-Publication Data
Hodder, Bridget.
    The rat prince / Bridget Hodder. — First edition.
        pages cm
    Summary: A new take on the Cinderella story, told from her point of view as
well as that of a royal rat turned coachman.
    ISBN 978-0-374-30213-9 (hardback) — ISBN 978-0-374-30214-6 (e-book)
    [1. Fairy tales. 2. Rats—Fiction. 3. Princes—Fiction. 4. Stepfamilies—
Fiction.] I. Title.

    PZ8.H64Rat 2016
    [Fic]—dc23

                                                              2015015073

Our books may be purchased in bulk for promotional, educational, or business
use. Please contact your local bookseller or the Macmillan Corporate
and Premium Sales Department at (800) 221-7945 ext. 5442 or by e-mail
at MacmillanSpecialMarkets@macmillan.com.

For Peter, for Richard, and for you, Claude—
with love, all things are possible

The Rat Prince

Prologue

When you hear the tale of Cinderella, do you ever wonder about the rats who were turned into coach-men by her fairy godmother?

No?

Then do take a moment to consider.

As the story goes, they were captured, twisted into human form by powerful magic, and tossed onto a coach that had, only seconds before, been a pumpkin.

Few pause to ask themselves how the rat-coachmen felt about all this. And no one seems to know what became of them afterward.

Were they frightened? In pain? Did they survive the experience? Upon reflection, you may even pity the poor creatures.

Don't.

We're faring quite well, I assure you.

Better than well, in my case. For there's more to the tale of Cinderella than has yet been revealed.

Now settle yourselves in comfort, and be sure you've plenty of provisions upon which to nibble, for you are about to hear the true story from Cinderella herself... and from me.

My name is Char.

In former days, they called me the Rat Prince.

Prince Char

You know her as Cinderella.

But before her stepmother came to Lancastyr Manor, the humans called her Rose de Lancastyr.

They also called her beautiful.

This confused my rat-subjects and me, since we found her painfully unattractive, with her huge salad-green eyes, skin like cream, and long waves of butter-yellow hair. Yet regardless of her looks and the fuss people made of them, Lady Rose was both gentle and kind. So after her mother died—and was replaced three months later by a wicked stepmother, Lady Wilhemina—we felt pity for the girl. We comforted her and came to consider her a rat-friend.

Though we believed her to be a lackwit.

For what kind of human makes friends with rats?

Apparently, the same kind who lets a stepmother turn her into a kitchen maid and give her the new, insulting name of Cinderella.

A lackwit.

However, one hot morning in early September, made hotter by the fragrant, ever-burning cedar fire in the flagstone kitchen of Lancastyr Manor, I discovered we were mistaken.

"Ahhhh, baking day," I murmured to my trusty royal councillor and best friend, Swiss. "Quite my favorite time of the week." A rich, yeasty aroma filled the kitchen and made my whiskers quiver as he and I peered through a crack in the door of a cupboard.

Swiss whispered back, "Oh, Your Highness, just look at that bread. I'll wager it's crisp at the top and chewy in the center. Cook may be a spiteful rat-killer, but she certainly has a way with a loaf."

We watched from our hiding place while Cook and the kitchen boy, Pye, pulled the last loaves from the brick oven. They set them to cool on a large rack against the wall, near a spot where Swiss and I had long ago loosened a board to provide easy rat-access to this marvelous treat.

Perfect.

"We'll come back tonight to thieve more," I said. "But let's try for a bit right away. If we move fast enough, we can bite some off, taunt Cook, and make our escape."

"Yes!" Swiss replied with enthusiasm, rather than trying to stop me, as a truly prudent royal councillor should have done.

I smiled to myself. "Watch and wait, then move upon my command."

Cook picked up a corner of her stained apron, wiped it across her sweaty pink forehead, and shouted, "Cinderella!"

That name distracted me from my designs upon the bread. I pressed my eye closer to the crack in the door, seeing Cook frown as she batted at her wiry gray hair, which stood out in frizzy corkscrews around her face.

She shouted for Cinderella again, then grumbled to Pye, "Drat her lazy bones! She's supposed to mix up a lemon potion to get rid of Miss Eustacia's freckles in time for the royal ball at Castle Wendyn on Saturday. Prince Geoffrey will choose a wife that night, and we've got to help our Miss Eustacia catch his attention!"

I stifled a laugh. If I knew anything about

humans—and I did—Lady Rose's older stepsister, Eustacia, would need a great deal more help than bleached freckles to attract the attention of a human prince. Nonetheless, the entire household and the stepmother, Lady Wilhemina, in particular, had been in a fever of anticipation for the past month, ever since the invitations had arrived. The king of Angland had invited the families of every eligible young lady in the capital city of Glassevale.

Pye remarked, "Poor Cinderella. She's had no rest, what with all the preparations for that fancy party." He was grimy and his homespun breeches were patched at the knees, but he had an intelligent look.

Cook gave a harsh laugh. "Ha! Are you in love with the wench, too? Menfolk are fools, from youngest to oldest, turned to corn mush by a smile and saucy cheeks."

"I'm not in love! You worked for Lady Wilhemina when she was married before—it's right strange you haven't noticed yet how hard she is on her servants." Missing the expression on Cook's face, the boy went on to mention Cook's rival, the housekeeper: "Mrs. Grigson says no servant ever left Lancastyr Manor willingly in the old days. The only one who left was my mam—and that's because she died! Now, since

Lady Wilhemina came, Mrs. Grigson says it's impossible to keep staff."

Alas, Pye was not as smart as he looked.

"Why, you lout! Never you mind what that hoity-toity Mrs. Grigson says! You pay Lady Wilhemina respect, or I'll box your ears!" Cook raised her big, gnarled hands in the air as if to follow through on her threat.

Pye ducked and ran to the other end of the cavernous room, huddling behind some sacks of cornmeal and dried beans. "Please don't," he begged. "I'm sorry."

Cook grunted and dropped her hands. "Then keep your trap shut. God's Bones, I'm worn out. Up since four o'clock of the morning mixing and kneading those loaves, and then having to send up breakfast in bed to everyone at the same time as the batches were ready for baking."

"Well, Cinderella and I helped," Pye said.

Poor lad. She would surely box his ears now, unless her attention was diverted. I switched Swiss with my tail. "The bread. Now!"

We darted out from the cupboard, deliberately running across Cook's toes and leaping up to the lowest shelf of the rack. We each bit off a mouthful of crust before jumping down and disappearing into a convenient hole under a baseboard in the hall. It opened onto a rat-passage through the walls, which we followed up and around and back into the same kitchen cupboard we'd been in before. And there we sat, crunching our heavenly crusts in high glee as we watched Cook shriek, grab a broom, and beat about the floor as if we were still underfoot and available for thwacking. "Nasty, dirty, vile brutes! Lady Wilhemina was right! We must buy more poison and kill them all!"

After a moment's hysterics, she calmed somewhat and barked at Pye, "You, boy, stop gaping like a looby and go find Cinderella. Get her back to work. For the Lord's sake, what a to-do! I think I'd best go snatch a quick nap."

We knew from past experience that Cook's "snatch a quick nap" meant "guzzle the cooking sherry in the privacy of my room." She had never before taken one of these naps so early in the day, but Swiss and I had given her something to recover from just now. Which meant we could make further incursions upon the bread if we waited until she left.

Cook's footsteps shuffled away, fading from our hearing. Pye sighed, emerged from behind the sacks, and made off in the other direction.

At last. Swiss and I let loose the laughter we'd been holding back, making such a noise that we didn't hear the other footsteps as they approached. Suddenly, the cupboard door flew open to reveal Rose de Lancastyr.

My laughter halted abruptly; Swiss squeaked like a mouse.

It was Rose's turn to laugh. "You rascals! I wondered who was causing such a rumpus. I should have realized—it's baking day, so where else would you be but the kitchen?"

I answered her seriously, though I knew she, like the rest of her kind, was ignorant of rat-speech. "The kitchen is where smart rats belong. But you are the rightful lady of Lancastyr Manor. What are *you* doing here?"

The kitchen was where Rose spent most of her days. Although she was no longer allowed to eat much food, she seemed to be constantly in the process of preparing it—chopping, stirring, kneading, peeling. And in her rare moments of leisure, she would sit near the fireplace upon her three-legged stool, warming her toes and watching Cook with unusual care.

We never thought much about why she did so. If you had asked me at the time, I might have said she was keeping an eye on the ill-tempered woman in order to avoid being hit with a ladle or a wooden spoon.

"You naughty Blackie," Rose said to me, smiling. "Always the leader of the rats' kitchen raids!"

I had no way of telling her my name wasn't Blackie, but Char, in honor of the way I like my meats— grilled over an open fire, with fat crackling, black as my royal fur. There was also no means of letting her know I was not just a leader of the rats of Lancastyr Manor, I was their one and only ruler, the prince of the Northern Rat Realm. My realm encompassed the entire northern half of the human city of Glasse-vale. The Southern Rat Realm was now ruled by Princess Mozzarella and had been established by an offshoot of the original rats of Lancastyr Manor long ago. It was made up of the southern half of the city and also included Castle Wendyn and its surround-ing estates.

Rose reached out and stroked the top of my head. "I need those lemons in that bowl behind you to whip up something for Eustacia. I think you'd better run along now."

Ignoring her patronizing tone, I leaned into her touch. I should have been far too conscious of my royal dignity to allow her to pet me thus. It almost placed me at the level of—dare I say it—a loathsome, purring cat. And yet I could not bring myself to put a stop to it.

"Your Highness," Swiss cautioned. "Let's go!"

I paid him no heed. This joyful petting might have continued for some time, had not Lady Wilhemina suddenly burst through the arched stone doorway.

We all froze.

Rose's skin suddenly became less the color of cream and more like the greenish tinge of skimmed milk. The only things moving on Swiss were his shivering whiskers.

I imagined I probably looked just as frightened as Swiss, though in reality what I felt was fury. For Wilhemina was our sworn rat-enemy; since her arrival the year before she had been waging a harrowing campaign against my people and me. We had lost several of our number—good rats and true—to her sly poisoning tactics.

"Cinderella!" she yelled.

The girl jerked her hand back and slammed the cupboard shut, plunging Swiss and me into safe darkness.

"Time to flee!" Swiss whispered. "Your Highness, what are you doing?"

"Peeking through the crack, of course. What does it look like I'm doing? Dancing the minuet?"

"But, my prince, if that woman finds us here we are surely doomed."

"Ha. If she dares lay a finger on me, I shall bite it off," I answered.

He jostled me a bit with his shoulder. "It is my responsibility to warn you when I think you're in danger."

"Be easy, Swiss. Wilhemina is not aware of our presence."

"And you call me your royal councillor," he grumbled. "When have you ever taken my advice?"

I ignored Swiss in favor of witnessing the scene unfolding in the kitchen.

Wilhemina towered over her stepdaughter. Her gown of robin's-egg blue silk rustled like the stealthy stir of a predator in the bushes. The elegance of her dress made Rose's tattered brown garment look even more shapeless than it had a moment before. The woman was doused in some sort of exotic perfume, drowning out the more pleasant scents in the room.

Swiss commented, "You must admit the stepmother's eyes are most alluring—small, dark, set close together. If you consider them along with her prominent nose, she appears almost ratlike."

"Very well, I admit it," I said with reluctance. "She's somewhat attractive. But her character is base."

"Lazy wench!" Wilhemina snarled at Rose. "Why is Eustacia still awaiting her bleaching potion? I told you to make it almost half an hour ago!"

Rose replied, "Do you not recall that you asked me to tend to the needs of my other sister, Jessamyn, first? I have only now come from her chambers."

Ah yes, Jessamyn—the younger, nicer stepsister.

"She is *Miss* Jessamyn to you, and no sister of yours!" Wilhemina shrieked and slapped her.

My tail stiffened, then slashed once behind me, like a whip.

One of the first things my mother had taught me in the days before I rose to rulership was how to control my temper. To plan my deeds, rather than react in the heat of the moment. So I did not spring into foolhardy action. I merely added the incident to the long list of things Wilhemina would someday regret.

"She will pay for that slap," I vowed. "When she least expects it, the woman will pay. I shall crunch her bones and suck out their marrow."

"Er, perhaps you should calm yourself, Prince Char," Swiss said, and sidled away from me.

Rose raised her hand to her cheek but kept her gaze toward the floor. Her tone was careful when she said, "There was no need to strike me. I've always done your bidding."

"Don't dare to argue with me, Cin-der-el-la!" Wilhemina snapped. The woman pronounced the syllables of the nickname slowly, insultingly.

"I apologize, ma'am," Rose said. There was no resentment in her voice, only the clear, harmonious tones of a well-bred young lady.

I was disappointed, as usual, in her response. No rat would have humbled herself thus before such a shrew.

But the girl's humility did not satisfy Wilhemina, who gave Rose a cold once-over with her eyes narrowed to slits. "Cinders in your hair, bare feet, dirty hands ... Who would think that folk once compared your beauty to your mother's? Though of course I never met the woman. Perhaps they called her Lady Jane the Lovely out of mockery rather than admiration."

Rose's fingers clutched a handful of her skirt till her knuckles whitened. "Your concern for my mother's reputation is most kind," she said. "I'm sure you've seen the portrait of her in the long gallery in the east wing of the manor. It is a good likeness." Then slowly, gracefully, Rose sank into a curtsy. She arched her long neck and stretched her arms behind her like a swan holding up its wings. I'd never seen a human female ever look quite so magnificently animal.

A curtsy that deep was meant to be performed only before royalty. Girls of the noble houses learned it before being presented for their debut at Castle Wendyn when they turned fifteen. We rats knew—in fact, the whole of Lancastyr Manor knew—that unlike Rose and her parents, Wilhemina and her daughters were not of noble blood and had never met the king or queen. This chewed away at Wilhemina's gut in much the way we rats would like to have done.

"My, my," said Swiss. "Now that is a curtsy."

Wilhemina's furious intake of breath betrayed that she, too, understood how her stepdaughter's gesture had shifted the balance of power between them back to Rose. She loomed up as if to strike the girl once more but halted when Rose finally raised her eyes, revealing a blaze of contempt so searing that even I was shocked by it.

Wilhemina sputtered briefly in the face of such

intensity. Then she seemed to recover herself. "Carry out my orders, wench. And in case you were stupid enough to be wondering, you will certainly not be going to the ball day after tomorrow." She turned to quit the room and spat over her shoulder as she went: "You shall regret your disrespect. I swear it."

Rose held the curtsy and waited until Wilhemina was gone before she whispered, "Not as much as you shall regret yours."

Then at last, I understood.

Rose de Lancastyr was not a lackwit at all.

Like me, she was biding her time.

CINDERELLA

When my stepmother left the kitchen, I rose from my curtsy and counted to ten before allowing my wobbly knees to give way. I kept myself from falling by catching the smooth warm wood of a table behind me with the heels of my hands. Then I felt a surge of rage in my breast. For a moment I let myself imagine revenge upon Wilhemina, picturing ways of making her suffer for the things she'd done to me, my father, and the pride of my family lineage.

Suddenly Pye appeared, panting as if he'd been running up and down stairs. "Lady Cinderella, I was looking for you all over the manor. You seem overset—is something wrong?"

After taking a few deep, shuddering breaths, I was

able to reply. "Thank you for your concern, dear Pye. I am quite well."

"But your cheek . . ." He reached out a hand.

"Never mind me, Pye. I will be fine. You should return to your duties, or Cook will scold." I stood taller, placed a hand lightly upon his shoulder, and steered him toward the scullery.

I felt sympathy and shame that this boy—the orphan of our former kitchen maid, who had been supported by my parents until my mother's death—was now forced to work so hard at such a young age. If I ever succeeded in getting my stepmother out of Lancastyr Manor, I would see that Pye was allowed to enjoy a true childhood.

Yet at the moment I could do nothing but watch his bent head and dragging steps as he walked away.

I turned toward the table and leaned upon it, still trying to quiet my limbs, which always shook after Wilhemina struck me. I could not dwell in this moment any longer without giving rein to destructive anger, so I closed my eyes and forced myself to think of the happy days before Wilhemina came to Lancastyr Manor.

Seventeen years had passed since my birth, and almost sixteen of them had been spent with a young mother who adored me, and with a father—twenty years older than her—who loved us both. In those days, Lancastyr Manor had rung with laughter and music and witty conversation at Mother's balls and soirées and garden parties.

With a sigh, I recalled curling up in the charmed circle of Mother's arms as the two of us shared secrets in the rumpled luxury of her chamber. The memory gave me comfort, so I sought more comfort by remembering how safe I'd once felt while learning to read and write at the knee of my father, Barnaby de Lancastyr. Oh, the cries of pride and delight Papa had given when I wrote my first letters on parchment, in great swirls of violet ink! My parents had taught me how to love and to learn.

But they had left out an important part of my schooling: what to do when your sweet mother dies in childbirth along with your baby brother. Nor had I been told how to cope when your father then loses his reason and, three months later, weds a wicked woman who threatens the Lancastyrs with ruin.

I tensed again.

Despite these gaps in my education, I was learning fast.

The Rose of those idyllic days had been thrust aside to make way for a new girl named Cinderella.

She was stubborn, watchful, desperate.

But she was not yet defeated.

I decided to look for my father and try once more to rouse him to action. He had a meandering, muddled mind, but upon occasion he took a brief turn for the better. Perhaps today would be one of his good days.

I meant to find out, just as soon as I mixed up the lemon concoction for my stepsister.

Later, after slathering the lemon potion on an ungrateful Eustacia, I found my father in the library, in his favorite upholstered chair, with a huge book upon his lap. He looked so peaceful it seemed wrong to disturb him. But I knelt by his side on the purple-and-blue Persian carpet and clutched his arm, hoping my timing was right.

"Papa, I know it's difficult for you, but please listen," I begged. "Things cannot continue as they are. I've written several times to your old friends Sir Tompkin and Lord Bluehart for help, but they haven't replied."

He kept his gaze on the pages in front of him, and when he spoke his tone was quite ordinary. "Have you heard, Daughter, that beyond the edge of the seas, there are dragons big enough to swallow a man alive? See here, in this atlas—they are painted in the margins of the maps." He gave a quizzical shake of his head and his curled white wig slipped a bit.

I reached up to set it aright.

"Oh. Thank you, my dear." He looked at me now, but there was no recognition in his stare. "Who might you be? You seem familiar. Is your name Lady Jane?"

A lump lodged in my throat. "I am your daughter, Rose. Lady Jane was my mother, your wife. I am told that I resemble her. She died a little over a year ago."

"No, no, girl, my wife is called Wilhemina," he corrected, with a forlorn expression. "I could never forget that!"

Who could?

"Please try to remember," I urged. "I am your only child."

"I thought I had others," he said vaguely.

When had so many lines appeared on my father's brow? Fretful lines of vain attempts to capture memories that had slipped away, off the edge of the world, perhaps, to be swallowed by the dragons lurking there.

I hoped they choked.

"I'm quite sure I have at least one other daughter," he continued.

"Eustacia?" I provided the name of my haughty elder stepsister with some bitterness.

"No, no . . . Let us consider, allow me to think . . ."

But all thought scattered, for at this instant my stepmother swept into the library. Her color was high. "There you are, Cinderella, you headstrong, disrespectful girl. Back to the kitchens!"

In as quiet and steady a voice as I could muster, I replied, "I have finished my given duties, and I simply desired to spend a moment with my father."

"I will endure no more of your disrespect. You will address me as *my lady*," Wilhemina insisted, her eyes ablaze. "Say it, Cinderella."

At this, my father seemed to revive. He sat up straight. The atlas fell unheeded to the floor. "That's it!" he roared.

"What, Papa?" I clasped his hand in mine, hoping against hope.

"Why, the name of my other daughter, of course," he declared with a smile. "Cinderella!"

No, no.

"Girl," he said to me then, "is something wrong with your cheek? It's a bit pink."

My stepmother's long mouth curved upward and she actually laughed, as if savoring her triumph. My father's comment had underscored the fact that with his mind constantly a-wander, she could continue to abuse the inhabitants of this house as she pleased.

"Get out," she said to me, dropping a hand onto my father's shoulder. "You're upsetting him."

"This is an outrage," I protested. "Papa, tell her she cannot send me away!"

"Oh dear, oh dear!" he exclaimed, tears welling up. "What is happening? Who are you, young lady, and why do you worry me so?"

Wilhemina said, with venom dripping from her tongue, "Cinderella, you simply must stop frightening Lord Lancastyr. You have more duties to perform. Eustacia and Jessamyn have laundry for you to collect and wash. And then, of course, there is the luncheon to prepare..."

My father hunched his shoulders, looked from Wilhemina to me, and began to cry piteously, like a child.

I could not prolong his pain or mine.

Though it tore my heart to do so, I quit the room.

In direct disobedience of Wilhemina's orders, I did not go to my stepsisters' chambers to collect their soiled garments and bring them to the laundry, where I would scrub my palms raw cleaning them.

At this moment, I *could* not.

Instead, up the servants' stairway I climbed, up and up and up, till the carpet ended and the wood of the steps became warped and splintered. At the very top of the stairs, a narrow corridor led to the small chamber where I now slept, one tiny part of the vast maze of attics in Lancastyr Manor. I sighed, pushed open my door, and threw myself upon my cot.

There were fourteen good bedchambers in my ancestral manse, but Wilhemina had moved Eustacia into my former suite and exiled me to this bare chamber. I hasten to add, the servants of Lancastyr Manor had most comfortable quarters in which to sleep. This was never meant to be a bedroom at all, but a boxroom; it was chokingly hot in summer and freezing in winter. If Mrs. Grigson had not given me several blankets and provided me with a small rug against Wilhemina's orders, I would have died of the cold in January of that first year.

I tightened my lips against another wave of hurt. Why on earth had those so-called friends of my

family, Sir Tompkin and Lord Bluehart, not inter-
vened before now—or even visited us? And why had
they ignored my repeated requests to meet with them?
Perhaps my letters had given them cause to think I
was a spoiled creature, jealous of a new stepmother.
If only I could be granted just a few moments alone
with them, to raise the question that had burned in
my breast for a year, ever since the afternoon my
father and I had met Wilhemina at the dressmaker's,
where we'd gone to buy my mourning gown: How
had her first husband died?

In the dressmaker's back parlor on that ill-starred
day, two ladies had been gossiping behind their hands
about a customer in the next room, a brass-faced
widow who had just moved to Glassevale from the
provinces. I overheard them saying that the circum-
stances of her husband's death were suspicious.

Later the same week, Wilhemina had appeared
uninvited with her daughters at my mother's funeral,
sitting in the back pew and putting on pious airs to
catch my father's interest. Shocked whispers had
floated through the quiet air of the church, whispers
about her dark past and her bold behavior.

Three months later, Papa—God help him!—had
married her.

I had repeated the gossip to him, but he would have none of it—further indication that his mind and wits were starting to slip.

Stuck here in servitude, I could do nothing to discover the facts. Meanwhile, my stepmother had ordered the servants to place rat poison throughout Lancastyr Manor. If any of it were to "accidentally" end up in my father's food or drink . . .

No. I shuddered to think of it. That would never happen, not so long as I kept up my vigil in the kitchen.

I was still caught up in these useless musings when I heard the creak of my door opening.

"Jessamyn!" I cried.

This was the first time my nine-year-old stepsister had ever ventured into the attic. She stood there on the rough floorboards in her pretty lavender day gown, glancing about the room with a horrified expression on her round face.

I hastened to enfold her in a hug. Her childish smell of powder and soap gave me strength somehow.

"You shouldn't have come up here, my dear," I said. "Your mother would be livid if she found out!"

She embraced me in return before declaring, "I was worried about you! I heard Mamma shouting in the library and I believed you must have fled to your chamber, so I crept up here ever so quietly. No one will miss me." Her lively face troubled, she gestured at the bare walls and sagging cot. "I don't like this awful place. *You're* the one who should not be here, Rose."

How could anyone as unloving and unlovely as my stepmother have brought forth someone as adorable as Jessamyn? Her father must have been a good man. Surely he'd deserved better than Wilhemina.

We sat down on my cot. It creaked, unsteady under our combined weight. With a hand so calloused by work I could hardly recognize it as my own, I smoothed back her brunette curls. Some of the fine hairs snagged on my rough skin. "Now then, Jessamyn, don't worry about me. It's not so terrible in the attic."

She wrinkled her nose.

"How can you say that?" she asked, tears brimming in her brown eyes. "What could be good about a place like this?"

I considered for a moment before I could summon a believable reply. "When I lie here, I can glance out my window and see the open sky, the sun in the morning and the stars at night." I gestured toward the tiny cracked windowpanes. "The view frees my heart to dream beautiful things."

"What do you dream about?" She sniffled, cuddling her head against my shoulder.

"Let me see," I said, smiling. Then the thought arose unbidden: *I dream of seeing your mother dragged from Lancastyr Manor in disgrace.* My smile faded. That would not do!

"Rose? Aren't you going to tell me what you dream about?"

I came up with a happy answer. "Every night, I have a vision of a handsome prince. He's clever, and dangerous to his foes, but not dangerous to me. He has black hair and dark eyes, and his crown shines like the stars in the sky. He comes to me and holds out his long, sensitive fingers and says—"

"Come away with me!" Jessamyn squealed.

I gave an involuntary spurt of laughter. "Yes! That's exactly what he says. How did you guess?"

"I have dreams like that, too," she said, solemn. "Does he marry you, your prince?"

"Yes. He marries me and takes me to a big palace with lots of servants who are very kindly treated, and I never have to scrub floors, or wash sheets, or burn my fingers on hot pans ever again," I said. "Though," I added, mindful of reality, "we must solve our own difficulties in life, not wait for others to do it on our behalf."

"If you meet Prince Geoffrey at the ball, perhaps you will marry him and move to a big palace," Jessamyn said, beaming.

I felt a secret pang of longing and regret. Though once I had attended balls and parties, it had been ages since I'd mingled in society. "Oh, Sister, I am not going to the ball. You must know that already. Kitchen girls do not dance with princes." The words caught involuntarily in my throat.

Jessamyn gave a small frown. "You are not a kitchen girl. The king invited you; I saw your name upon the card."

I was sure Wilhemina had already dreamed up an excuse for my absence from the ball that would satisfy any questioners. Would it be a sick headache? Or perhaps a putrid sore throat? I could think of any number of excellent ailments. "Jessamyn, surely you've noticed that since your mother married my father, I have not left the grounds of Lancastyr Manor."

"Mamma told me you're too sad to see anyone

since your own mamma died. I heard her telling her friend Lady Harriet that your mother's death had turned your mind, as it did your father's. I wasn't sure what she meant by that. Yet I'm very sorry you miss Lady Jane so much."

As she gave me a sympathetic kiss on the cheek, I tried not to grind my teeth. So that was Wilhemina's explanation for my disappearance from society! How neat were the knots with which she had tied me!

After a brief, uncomfortable silence, Jessamyn said with determined cheer, "The prince of my dreams doesn't marry me."

"Oh?"

"He just takes me away from Mamma. He gives me a fluffy white lapdog and bread and honey, as much of it as I like."

"When I become a princess, I'll arrange that for you," I assured her, with another smile to cover a sudden wave of despair. Then, thank goodness, I was distracted by a scrabbling sound. "Oh, look there!" I pointed. "It's Blackie and his friend Frump-Bum."

"Eeeeeeeeeeeek!" Jessamyn screamed and clung to me. "Rats, rats, *rats*!"

Had I truly become so removed from my old life

that I'd forgotten how most people would react to the presence of rodents?

Yes.

"Don't be afraid, Jessamyn! They aren't ordinary rats!"

She gasped, and almost choked me in her embrace. "They certainly look like them."

Poor Blackie and Frump-Bum stood stock-still on their hindquarters, as if assessing the danger from the mad creature on the cot. They were odd, these friendly rats. You'd think they'd have scurried away as fast as they could.

"No," I said. "They're not rats, but pets. I play with them, and they with me. They are tame."

"Truly? How can that be?" By her tone, I could tell Jessamyn was not convinced.

"My father used to say the rats of Lancastyr Manor have always been extraordinary beasts. In fact, when your mother makes me go without meals, they bring me leftovers from the table. Meat pasties, fruit, cakes, bread . . ."

Jessamyn's plump lips formed an *O* of astonishment, as Blackie and Frump-Bum continued to watch us.

"There's something else about my pets," I said. "When your mother first sent me up here, I was very lonely. One night I was crying, and I heard a scuffling noise. I wondered what it could be."

"Was it the rats?"

"It was Blackie. I was not afraid of him, even though my old nursemaid used to tell me stories about how rats would eat the faces of sleeping babies if you didn't guard their cradles."

"Oh!" Jessamyn clearly hadn't heard this old wives' tale before. Her bottom lip started to tremble.

"It's not true, of course," I hastily added. "Just an ignorant tale." Though I was not quite sure.

"Tell me more of what your father said about the Lancastyr rats being special," she said.

"He'd heard about the rats as a boy, from his grandfather. Something about them being intelligent or long-lived . . . different in some way. I have forgotten exactly. My mother laughed when my father spoke of it, and he became embarrassed and did not raise the subject again. However, lately I wonder if there was truth in what he said."

Jessamyn gave an impatient bounce. The rats inched forward and stopped. "Why?"

"Well, that night when I was so unhappy, Blackie padded right up to my bed and did the strangest thing." I stopped, remembering.

Jessamyn stared at me.

I hesitated, then decided to tell the whole truth. "Why, he . . . he had something in his mouth. Something that glinted in the moonlight. He made a little noise, like nothing I'd ever heard from a rat, and then he sat up, took the object out of his mouth, and handed it over."

Yes, Blackie had "handed" it to me, though he did not exactly have hands.

"What was it?"

I reached under the bodice of my homespun dress, where I had hidden the thing in a pocket of my muslin shift. I pulled it out and cradled it in my palm so she could see, but not touch.

"A ring!" she exclaimed.

Yes. It was a large sapphire, set in heavy, soft, almost pink gold. Etched across the surface of the jewel was a coat of arms.

"It has a carving on it," my stepsister breathed in awe.

"The seal of the Lancastyrs," I said.

Together, on the same impulse, Jessamyn and I raised our eyes to look over at the rats.

They were nearer now.

Blackie's dark gaze on me was so intent, I would almost swear he understood what I'd said.

"But where could the rat have gotten such a thing?"

Jessamyn demanded. "Wait. You're merely teasing me, aren't you? Oh, Rose, how could you?"

"I'm not teasing! Blackie gave me the ring. And every time I feel discouraged or tired or hungry, I touch it, and somehow it gives me the strength to carry on."

"Don't let my mother see it," Jessamyn said, in her wise little voice.

She was right, of course. I tucked it away again, out of sight.

Prince Char

I wanted to nudge Rose's arm and tell her not to fear—if her stepmother were ever to steal the ring, I would get it back. Believe me when I say there is nowhere a rat cannot go, and there is certainly nowhere Lady Wilhemina could have hidden the ring where I wouldn't have found it. We rats had cherished the shiny golden thing for more than a century, ever since Prince Gravy, a most canny rat-ruler, nicked it from the bedside table of a slipshod Lancastyr ancestor, Vern the Vapid.

Swiss was looking at me with reproach in his eyes. "You have yet to explain why you gave our greatest treasure to a human."

"Our people have been linked to her family for

untold generations," I replied. "I know I can't explain the history or significance of the ring to her, but I thought it might at least bring her comfort and courage."

"Humph. We know the courage part didn't work," Swiss said. "And now that she has the thing, she'll keep it."

"Rose deserves it. She works hard, as hard as a rat. She could have been one of us."

"But she's not. She's human, and so she will stay," he pointed out, quite reasonably.

Without thinking, I rounded on him and nipped his hindquarters.

"Ow! What did you do that for?" He rubbed the sore place with his snout.

I wasn't sure myself, so I kept silent.

The younger girl, Jessamyn, cried out. "They're fighting!"

"Oh, no." Rose smiled at her. "Do you see, Frump-Bum didn't bite him back? Blackie had good reason to do that, you may be sure. He's the leader."

I said to Swiss in a jesting tone, "Take heed of what she says. And as your leader, I've been thinking about the upcoming ball—the one being given for the human prince, Geoffrey."

"The humans have been blathering about it for weeks," Swiss said, "but it's of no interest to us. Why, Castle Wendyn lies deep in the Southern Rat Realm of Princess Mozzarella. Even if we were to travel there, we would have to ask her permission for everything we took from the royal tables."

I cocked my ears back in exasperation. "I'm not speaking of a raid on the party food. Think, Swiss! Prince Geoffrey is seeking a wife. And you just heard Lady Rose say she would like a prince for a husband. Let us use our considerable capabilities to make it happen."

He gaped at me. "Your Highness, have you lost your wits? Your duty is to rats, not humans."

"I'm in full possession of my faculties. If Lady Rose were to marry the future ruler of Angland, she would remove Wilhemina from Lancastyr Manor forever. We would see an end to the poisonings." *And Lady Rose's eyes would shine once more with happiness.*

Swiss's eyes certainly shone at this. His ears perked up and his brown fur fluffed out like a mink's. "Oh, I see now. Excellent! Let's get started! Er, what can we do exactly?"

"Patience," I cautioned. "I must get a look at

39

Geoffrey first. And let us keep this notion of Rose marrying him to ourselves for the time being. I have no wish to give our people hope of ousting Wilhemina until I am sure it might actually come to pass."

I then heard Jessamyn ask Lady Rose, "What are they doing now? How cute that smaller one is, the brown one. Look at his cheeks. How they move as he squeaks!"

Rose replied, "Oh, no doubt they're saying something important. Now watch this." She inched forward. What was she up to? She put out her hand, and I quickly closed the space between us to sniff her fingers. They held the scent of pine soap, traces of bread and grease, and the other scent, pure Rose de Lancastyr—unique, indefinable.

"He will bite you!" the silly creature on the bed exclaimed.

"No, he won't," Rose said.

Then she moved her fingers to the back of my head and stroked my fur. I swayed from side to side with the rhythm until Swiss broke the spell.

"She's bewitching you!" he cried. "Let's be away! Now, Your Highness!"

I allowed him to persuade me. I thought perhaps he was right.

"All bow!" the majordomo boomed as I appeared in the doorway of my throne room to deliver my weekly royal speech. "Make way for his Royal Highness, Prince Char of the Northern Rat Realm; his royal mother, Lady Apricot; and his royal councillor, Swiss!"

My subjects put their snouts to the floor while I led the procession into the princely stronghold. It had been built by my people centuries before in a walled-off corner of an attic storeroom the Lancastyrs had long since forgotten.

Here was the throne of the prince.

And it was mine.

I adjusted my cape of royal purple, which was encrusted with sparkling amethyst on the back. Then I walked between rows of my bowing subjects, drawing satisfaction from surveying the piles of royal plunder leaning against the walls. We'd collected it from humans over the centuries: coins, jewels, rich clothing, gold goblets, silver buckles, and on and on, everything gleaming, colorful, textured. The treasure had been chosen to please our eyes, stimulate our senses, and delight our hearts.

After touching as many of my people as I could

with my tail, I left my lady mother and Swiss seated on two silk pillows, and came to a standstill before a window.

Light streamed in through the diamond-cut pane of leaded glass, illuminating my polished silver throne. The humans who had crafted this throne of beauty, molding it with intricate vines, fruits, and faces, had thought they were making a lavish bowl for serving soup. Ha, ha! With a plump velvet cushion stuffed inside it, where the soup used to be, the bowl was the perfect size and shape for the prince of the rats.

I sat upon it and gave my subjects a fond glance.

"My fellow rodents," I intoned, "I have aught to teach and tell. Recall that millennia ago, we rats came in the holds of Phoenician ships to the shores of this island country, which the humans call Angland, led by the great Prince Feast. In each succeeding generation, by winning our traditional trials of wit and skill, only the strongest and wiliest of rats have become prince of the Northern Rat Realm, as have I."

"Wise one! Noble one!" The pleasing epithets blew about the room at my feet.

It's good to be prince.

I raised my voice again. "Every day, I concern myself with your safety, and with the important thing, the essential thing, the main goal of every true leader..." I let my voice trail off, to invite the traditional chant.

"*Food.* Find the Food! *Food.* Find the Food!" the crowd shouted in a most satisfactory chorus.

"Our realm is under threat," I declared. "As each one among you is aware, Wilhemina wants no rat left alive in Lancastyr Manor. I have already warned you of the dangers of choice food left lying inexplicably upon the floor. That is how we lost our dear companions Crust, Mince, Strawberry, and Trout last year. Lately, Cook has begun scattering poison among the crumbs she drops between table and wall, the better to deceive us. And thus were murdered the three small daughters of Gulp and Grill, and two of our mouse friends, Erasmus and Hermia. But we will not fall victims again to such trickery, I vow!"

"Hear, hear!" the majordomo said in a loud, mellifluous voice. "Prince Char has given his royal word!"

Sadness brought on by the mention of our dearly departed settled over the room. I allowed a moment of respect and remembrance. Yet we could not dwell upon our losses without planning action to prevent more.

I twirled my whiskers. "Take heart. Since Royal

Councillor Swiss and I set up a watch to keep Cook and Wilhemina under surveillance at every hour of the day or night, we have not lost a single one of our number to poison. We are also working upon ways to rid ourselves of Wilhemina forever. Our people will flourish. We will keep the Food safe and pure!"

I made a wide arc with my tail, and the gathering responded: "*Food.* Find the Food!"

"Good folk of the Northern Realm, I must tell of another potential threat. It comes once again from the humans, but this time, from those outside Lancastyr Manor."

There was a rumble of unease.

I resumed my speech. "Though human rule encompasses all of Angland and includes the land upon which both the Northern and Southern Rat Realms rest, the humans allow their throne, this great responsibility, to pass from parent to oldest child without any tests of worthiness. Such a foolish practice has led to many an incompetent human king or queen causing trouble for rat-kind. Unlike the current human ruler, Good King Tumtry of Angland, the bad sort of ruler ignores his or her duty to the Food. Who could forget what our histories tell of Ablered the Awful, or Queen Millicent the Mad?"

I paused to inhale deeply. I could tell by their scents that my people were indeed recalling with horror the tales of past bad human rulers.

"My friends, surely you have heard gossip in the sewers and the streets and the servants' quarters: Good King Tumtry is aged and ill. When he dies, his son, Geoffrey, will rise to the throne."

Chattering broke out. A small golden rat put up a nervous tail and asked, "Your Highness, is Geoffrey the sort of human you've just warned us about? The kind who doesn't look after the Food?"

"A wise question, madam!" I nodded. "I do not know the answer, and that is the problem. We must learn more about the heir to the throne, to find out how his kingship will affect us. Will we need to lay aside stores of grain and dried meats in enough quantities to stave off a famine? Is he a rat-enemy who will try to decimate our population? We cannot plan for the future until we know what the future holds."

"Hear, hear!" the majordomo called. "His Royal Highness, Prince Char, has spoken!"

Others took up the cry: "Hear, hear!"

I waited for silence, then announced: "On the day after tomorrow, when the big ball will take place,

Prince Geoffrey will surely be present at Castle Wendyn, awaiting the evening's event. Therefore, I shall lead a party of my most stalwart subjects across the city and into the castle that morning, to observe him and those around him. We shall discover the answers to all our questions. Who among you wishes to join our mission?"

"Me! Choose me, Your Highness!" My people pushed forward, their faces avid with excitement.

"Calm, my friends. Consider carefully before you volunteer for this venture. We must leave the Northern Rat Realm and cross over into the Southern Rat Realm. It will be dangerous."

This did not seem to daunt the clamoring crowd. I was glad our ancestors had thought to pack the walls of the throne room with straw, to deaden the passage of sound. For if Wilhemina could hear us, danger would surely follow.

I twirled my whiskers for a moment, then pointed to five of our very bravest citizens: "Truffle, Corncob, and over there in the back, the three Beef brothers," I declared. "You are the chosen ones."

They grinned and glowed as their companions cheered and twined tails with them in congratulations.

I commanded with a benevolent smile, "Go now, my subjects, and return to your daily tasks. My royal councillor and I must have quiet in which to contemplate our next moves."

As they dispersed, Swiss said in an undertone, "Well done, Your Highness. I'm sorry I doubted you earlier. But I still can't imagine how you propose to put a human girl on a human throne."

"The way I see it," I mumbled, "if we can get Prince Geoffrey to take one look at Rose, it's in the bag. Haven't you noticed? Every human male who sees her falls in love with her. Why, Mrs. Grigson has to go out every morning with her broom and shoo away young men who linger in the bushes in hopes of catching a glimpse of her, even though it's been ages since Rose has set foot outside the house."

Just then we were interrupted by my mother, who drew me aside with a grave, cautious touch upon my back. Her two favorite courtiers, Lady Lambchop and Lady Pudding, hovered right behind her.

"There is a word you left out of your speech today, Prince Char," she said. "And the word is *Cinderella*."

I did not like to hear my mother use that name for Rose, but I said nothing.

Swiss leaned in closer to eavesdrop. I poked him

hard with the tip of my tail. "Mother, I hardly think this is the time or the place to discuss these matters."

She twitched a whisker at her ladies, who minced away. Then she nosed me into a corner behind a heap of stolen ribbons and lace where no one—not even Swiss, who was straining hard—could hear us. I could smell her mood, which was tense and uncertain.

"My son, there are rumors about you and this Cinderella person. I cannot help but wonder if your sudden interest in the wider world of the human kingdom—all this talk of Good King Tumtry, and an expedition to Castle Wendyn—has something to do with that girl. Some say you are bespelled."

"I am not," I said.

"Then explain, my son. I am listening."

"I have a feeling about Rose. I think she's important to us."

"Stuff and nonsense. She's no longer of importance in her own home, to her own father. Char, if your sainted father were here today, he would be just as disapproving of your enthusiasm for her as I am."

I never knew my father, who had died on a failed mission to roll home a barrel of wine before I was born. Yet Lady Apricot invokes him every time we have a disagreement.

I took a deep breath before replying. "Mother, think for a moment of how dire things could get if Geoffrey turns out to be a bad king and drives the city to starvation. We would be obliged to leave Lancastyr Manor and go live in the countryside, making nests in bushes or cold stone walls. Scavenging in the woods."

There was a pause, filled with the vibrations of Lady Apricot's alarmed contemplation of this prospect. "Why do you wish to frighten me thus?" she said at last.

"Because you asked why I'm preoccupied with Lady Rose. If Geoffrey turns out to be a bad king, a good queen could counterbalance him, and save the country. An intelligent queen. A queen who has been forced to work hard, who has often gone hungry, who understands the primacy of the Food. A queen who has been kept alive by the Rat Prince."

Even as I spoke, I realized there was a problem with my rapidly developing scheme: It seemed a bit of hard luck on Rose that the worse Prince Geoffrey turned out to be, the more crucial it was (from the rat point of view) that she marry him. I felt for the poor girl.

Though I would never say so in front of Lady Apricot.

My mother's expression became thoughtful. "I begin to take your meaning, my son. You are thinking of Rose de Lancastyr becoming queen."

"None other. Consider her the rat candidate, if you will. Were I to succeed in placing a queen upon the human throne who is sympathetic to rat-kind, and who will free us from the dread Wilhemina, I shall have done a deed worthy of the great Prince Feast himself. But tell no one of this yet," I added hastily, well aware of how much my mother liked to chatter with her handmaidens. "We should not raise hopes prematurely."

Particularly since I still had no actual strategy of how to bring any of this about. But I was sure I'd come up with something.

Lady Apricot flared her nostrils and gave an abrupt switch of her tail. I could see her turning the idea over and over in her mind.

I also could see Swiss. He obviously understood by our postures and our scents that something momentous was being discussed, so he was creeping closer and closer.

"Oh, botheration, Swiss, you may join us," I called.

"I am your chief adviser, after all," he reminded me, taking his customary place by my side. "What's in the wind?"

"It's about Rose. I've told my mother our plans for her," I informed him.

He stepped backward and shook out his fur into spikes as if it had gotten wet. "You told *Lady Apricot* our secret?"

My mother ignored Swiss, to put him in his place. "My son, the idea is brilliant. How do you propose to fulfill these ambitions?"

I hid my lack of certainty with bold speech. "We must find a way for Rose to go to the prince's ball."

"But Wilhemina won't allow it," Swiss objected. "She said so in the kitchen this morning, do you not recall?"

"Of course, we must keep our ears to the walls and figure something out," I told Swiss.

Just then a chorus of squeaks and the pitter-patter of many tiny feet heralded the arrival of visitors: our local mice.

"Your Highness! Your Highness!" they cried as they approached.

My mother edged away from the flood of small creatures, curling her tail tight so none of them would tread upon it and sitting up tall on her haunches to emphasize the fact that she considered mice ill-mannered and pert. I myself am rather charmed by their small size and wee fluting voices, and must occasionally squelch an urge to scoop them up and hug them like nestlings.

Pompey, the head mouse, showed his respect by running in a circle, then came to rest directly in front of me and saluted. He gave a special little wave to my mother, who put her nose in the air.

"Yes, Pompey?" I nodded, with due courtesy. "Have you anything to report in our common cause against Wilhemina?"

Perhaps I ought to explain that mice require so little in the way of sustenance, they are content to eat the rats' leftovers—and in return for the food, they are quite useful to us as spies and allies.

He bowed his head and said, "Your Highness, my people and I were eavesdropping on your speech just now, and we took special note of your concern about the human prince."

His mention of eavesdropping caused no surprise for us, nor shame on his part, for all the animals who dwell in Lancastyr Manor keep a close watch upon each other—as is only proper and natural.

Pompey then said, with a little hop, "After you finished, some of my folk hastened to inform me that Lady Wilhemina—"

"Do not call her a lady," my mother snorted. "She is no such thing."

I paid no heed to Mother's rude interruption. "Continue, Pompey," I encouraged him. "What did your mice say?"

"Wilhemina is in Eustacia's bedchamber, and they are arguing about Prince Geoffrey right now," he said. "They talk of him often, but this time they're getting rather heated. Is that of interest to you?"

"Interest! Interest!" the other mice shrilled, skipping about until Pompey shushed them.

"I rather think it is," I replied. "Thank you." I untied my splendid royal cape and laid it aside with care, then turned to Swiss. "Shall we go?"

"Not without me," Lady Apricot insisted, and I saw no reason to protest.

The mice scattered before us as we leapt into action.

Across the floor, through the walls, and down the dormers we flew, arriving swiftly at Eustacia's bedchamber. In one corner, concealed by the legs of a bureau, was a comfortable spying-space behind the baseboard.

No particular precautions were necessary as we approached our vantage point, since Eustacia was shouting loud enough to frizzle one's fur: "I will be a failure at the ball!"

Rats have sharp ears, as you may be aware, so it was quite painful to listen.

She screamed again: "And furthermore, Mamma, I simply cannot abide this dress!"

Lady Apricot shied away from the noise, but Swiss and I pressed our faces to the spy-slit.

Wilhemina was seated upon an upholstered settee near the dressing table. And there was Eustacia standing in front of her, decked out in a fine gown, the exact hue of ripe zucchini at its greenest. Though the color was impressive, the dress did not suit her; it brought an unhealthy look to her skin, and the tiers of ruffles made her appear a bit like a cake would if its frosting slid down to settle around its base. However, I do not claim to be a judge of female garments.

A ladies' maid was crouched at her feet, putting pins into the hem of the skirt.

Wilhemina's voice was cold when she answered. "Be silent, Daughter. How many times must I reassure you? The dress is magnificent. Surely you will attract Prince Geoffrey's attention."

"Not in this hideous thing! I told you the yellow gown would flatter me more!" Eustacia folded her arms across her ample chest and aimed a kick at the ladies' maid.

"Ow!" cried the poor young woman, sitting back on her heels and spilling the pins hither and yon.

"Clumsy, useless wench!" Eustacia shrilled.

The maid ran from the room crying.

Wilhemina drawled, "Come now, my dear, do refrain from driving away yet another of the servants. I'll have a terrible time replacing her. If you continue in this manner, you'll end with no one but your stepsister to maid you. And, frankly, she's no good at it. Lord Lancastyr has spoiled her horribly. She has no useful skills whatsoever."

Eustacia stamped one foot on the polished oak parquet. "Mamma, you know full well I am not the only one who frightens away the servants. Why, when the butler gave notice, he said it was because he would not stay in any household of which you were mistress."

"Watch your tongue, ungrateful girl. We could retain staff if we had enough coin to throw at the problem, but I have already spent most of Lord Lancastyr's fortune," said Wilhemina. "Mind you, Eustacia, I've gone to all sorts of expense, decking you out in Zhinese velvet and South Sea pearls, with nothing to show for it. You still have not received any offers of marriage. So I expect you to be on your very best, most winning behavior at the ball."

Swiss's whiskers tickled my ear. "I wonder why no one wants her, eh? With her irresistible charm and character."

Eustacia thrust out her lower lip farther. "It is not my fault that I have no suitors, Mamma. I make myself agreeable to the gentlemen, laugh at their jests, touch their sleeves to show interest, and hang upon their every word."

Wilhemina's eyes had grown wider and wider during her daughter's speech. "Why, you foolish girl! Gentlemen are not interested in young ladies who exhibit desperate behavior. Ignore and torment the pitiful fools—that will bring them panting after you. It has always worked for me."

She glanced into the large gilded looking glass on Eustacia's dressing table, then frowned and touched an area under her chin experimentally. It wobbled.

I experienced a twinge of satisfaction at her startled look.

Eustacia threw herself upon her frilly bed. "But, Mamma, that is not what you did with Lord Lancastyr. I distinctly recall how, after you first encountered him at the dressmaker's, you constantly dragged us over to see him and even sent round a copy of the Reverend Throckmorton's *Book of Sermons on the Indubitable Promise of Heaven for the Souls of the Dearly Departed.*"

"Yes, well, that was different. When I met Lord Lancastyr, I could tell he was beginning to wander in his wits. I needed to move quickly if I was to snare him."

I felt my fur prickle at this cold-blooded admission that Wilhemina had never loved Rose's unfortunate father. Even my mother gave a twitter of surprise.

But the self-centered Eustacia did not seem to register Wilhemina's perfidy. "Never mind that," she said. "I've something more pressing to ask. Why did I hear you tell my stepfather that Cinderella will go to meet the prince with the rest of us?"

Her mother raised one thin shoulder in an elaborate shrug. "He saw the invitation with the spoilt wench's name included, and asked me about it. Since he was having a lucid moment, I dared not upset him." Then she stood up. "Besides, Daughter, you really ought to stop looking upon Cinderella as a rival. Have you not noticed she has become far less beautiful lately? Her skin has grown rough. Her eyes have purple shadows under them."

"That's not sufficient to make her ugly enough to discourage the prince if he saw her," Eustacia groused.

My mother squeezed closer to the viewing slot. "Ugly enough?" she echoed in anger. "How dare she speak thus of the rat-candidate for queen?"

"Sssh." I nudged her with my nose, though I felt the same rising fury myself.

Wilhemina spoke again. "Now, where has Jessamyn gone? It's almost time for luncheon." She turned and looked around as if Jessamyn might somehow have been in the room with them all along. "I declare, I quite despair of your sister sometimes. She disappears often, and I find her ensconced in odd corners of the house . . . *reading books.*"

"Reading!" Eustacia gasped. "How strange! That's what Cinderella used to do, before you put her to work."

Wilhemina picked up a swan's-down powder puff from the vanity table and lightly plied it over her cleavage. "Yes, well, I put a stop to that, didn't I? Idle hands are the devil's tools."

Swiss and I exchanged glances.

Eustacia suddenly sat up straight. "Hold on a moment, Mamma. How do you plan to keep Cinderella home from the ball? What if my stepfather remembers and demands she attend?"

Wilhemina gave one of her frigid smiles in response. "Why, the poor, sweet girl hasn't a thing to wear."

A nasty grin spread across Eustacia's face.

"So that's her game," I whispered to Swiss.

My mother turned away from the crack and faced us both. Her moon-white fur was ruffled with emotion. "The rat-candidate for queen shall appear before the human prince wearing garments more fine and costly than any other woman, taken from among the treasures of the Northern Rat Realm," she declared. "My son, the Rat Prince, will see to it."

"Not to disagree with you, Lady Apricot," Swiss said, "but I think *you* should see to it. Prince Char has no dress sense. Think of that ridiculous cape he wears to ceremonies."

CINDERELLA

The next day passed in a flurry of mad activity. I cooked, cleaned, and flew from chamber to chamber on errands. When at last dinner was finished and the plates cleared away, I found it almost restful to kneel upon the floor in the kitchen to scour at the places where grease had slopped from the cooking pans.

With each scrub, I imagined I was wiping Wilhemina from my life.

"Lady Rose!"

I looked up, startled. It was Mrs. Grigson, the housekeeper.

"Please stop cleaning the floor," she begged, her kind face soft with worry. "You'll ruin your poor knees. And your hands! If dear Lady Jane were alive to see this, her heart would be broken. Mine is, indeed."

"Thank you for your concern," I replied. "But someone must tidy up, and Pye is washing dishes in the scullery." Someone also had to collect and dispose of the poisoned scraps of meat Cook had left lying temptingly about as rat bait.

I put the scrub brush down for a moment to push the curls off my forehead where they'd escaped their clumsy topknot and looked up at Mrs. Grigson. Only then could I see the distress in her honest eyes.

I was not the only one for whom Wilhemina's arrival at Lancastyr Manor had spelled heartbreak.

"Don't worry about me," I said, smiling with an effort. "Your task is harder than mine: trying to keep the manor running since . . . since—"

"Since *that creature* bewitched your father!"

"Sssh, Mrs. Grigson! Cook is in her rooms, but she could be back at any time, and you know how sensitive she is about Wilhemina."

"Sensitive? Ha! She's a fine one, that Cook," Mrs. Grigson said bitterly, her chin thrust forward. "Brought here by Lady Wilhemina from her home in the country to replace our good cook Mrs. Benjy without so much as a by-your-leave! Everyone says Cook spies for her high-and-mighty ladyship and tattles when we complain."

"That's why you shouldn't be speaking to me. You

know the only reason you haven't been discharged yet is that you are willing to remain in spite of the fact that she has not paid you wages for months, and you put up with her evil temper."

Mrs. Grigson dabbed a shaking knuckle at the wrinkled corner of one eye. "You have the right of it. I tolerate her behavior because I must keep my place here. I'm too old to make my way afresh in the world. And you, child—I must look after you. But regardless of that, I had a reason to seek you out just now, my lady. Your stepmother has asked to see you in her chambers."

"Oh!" Was the sudden shaking in my breast fear? Or anger? Whatever it was, it haunted me daily.

I dropped the brush into the bucket, rose, and used my coarse skirt to dry my hands. "Very well. I shall go at once."

Mrs. Grigson stepped closer and extended her hands toward me as if to touch my shoulders, then let them fall. She took a deep breath. "My lady, you mustn't give in to your stepmother any longer. You must find the courage to stand up to her."

"Mrs. Grigson," I said quietly, "do you believe I am a coward for not defying Wilhemina?"

"Of course not!" she said, but her tone was unconvincing. "I understand that you're a gentle thing, my lady, and not bred to deal with the likes of such a woman. But it is your right to be treated with honor, as the true daughter of the house. Will you reflect upon that, for my sake?"

I nodded, unable to speak, though I longed to tell her the truth.

She dropped a kiss on my forehead. "Blessings upon you, Lady Rose, and luck."

I suppose I ought to have been insulted by her familiarity, yet it was so long since anyone had handled me gently, with love, that I felt a sorrowful weakness wash through me.

Mother, Mother. Why did you leave me here all alone?

Oh, no. This would never do. One kiss from the kindly housekeeper, and I come apart at the seams like one of Eustacia's overstuffed dresses? No. I had to be strong for my father, for Jessamyn, and for Mrs. Grigson herself.

I squared my shoulders and went upstairs. I wondered what fresh torment Wilhemina had dreamed up for me. Nothing she could devise would surprise me now . . .

Or so I thought.

Minutes later, I stumbled from Wilhemina's chamber in confusion, closed the door, and leaned back against it. I tried to catch my breath and somehow make sense of what had just occurred. Then I heard someone whisper my name.

"*Pssst.* Rose!"

I looked around.

It was Jessamyn, of course. She peeked from behind the stiff brocade curtains of a nearby window seat, her brown locks twining down the front of a pink satin gown. "Rose, over here!"

"Sister!" I ran down the hallway and threw my arms about her. "You'll never believe what your mother told me!"

"Quiet—I don't want *her* to find us!" She drew me behind the curtains and pulled me down onto the red-upholstered window seat. It was after seven o'clock and the sky outside was finally drawing down into dusk, but a brace of candles upon the window ledge flickered an unsteady light. "What did Mamma say? I heard from Mrs. Grigson that you'd been summoned, so I brought a book up here and waited."

"I'm going to the ball tomorrow!" I exclaimed. "Your mother has changed her mind. I can't believe it. In fact, I shouldn't believe it."

At first I'd been suspicious as to why Wilhemina would suddenly allow me to leave the manor, after all these months of keeping me confined here. However, she'd shown me the king's invitation with my name on it and said she was worried about awkward questions were I not to attend. Her begrudging tone had seemed quite genuine, and I was convinced.

At last—an opportunity to further my family's interests.

Jessamyn bounced up and down on the cushions. "Oh, Sister! Do you mean you have gotten over your reluctance to venture forth from home?"

I flinched at this reminder of Wilhemina's falsehood but decided to let it pass. "I do still mourn my mother, yet I am quite ready to emerge from this long isolation and see people once more," I assured her. And though it was not the full story, this was true enough.

Jessamyn clapped her hands. "We'll meet the prince together!"

"A dream come true," I whispered, though it was not romance I was thinking of. If my parents' old friends were at the ball, I would finally be able to explain my father's plight and enlist their aid.

And even if Sir Tompkin and Lord Bluehart proved uninterested, I could still catch the ear of either Prince Geoffrey or Good King Tumtry. Surely, after all the faithful service the Lancastyrs had given the Crown over the centuries, the prince or the king would be willing to find my father a physician and keep my stepmother from plunging us into ruin.

Jessamyn kissed me. "The prince will fall instantly in love with you. How could he not? You are the prettiest girl in the kingdom."

"Thank you, my little flatterer." I laughed in spite of myself. "Beauty may inspire interest, but that is not the same as love. And speaking of beauty, did I ever tell you I saw Prince Geoffrey once, long ago? It was when I went to the royal palace for my debut and met Queen Monette."

"You met Queen Monette before she died?" Jessamyn breathed, her face aglow. "Oh my! Was she nice?"

"Very. But she was aging and looked unwell."

Jessamyn paused for a moment. But she soon recovered and asked, "What does the prince look like?"

"He doesn't have dark hair like the prince of my dreams, but he's magnificent nonetheless." I closed my eyes, the better to remember. Then, ignoring my own wise advice about beauty that I had just dispensed to Jessamyn, I said in a swoony voice: "He has golden hair and golden eyes ... Perhaps they are evidence of a golden heart."

I couldn't help but wonder what it would be like to dance with such a man. To feel the warmth of his smile dawn upon my face, to be aware of his touch on my back as he guided me through the steps of an allemande or a minuet, swaying to the music of a royal orchestra.

Aloud, I said, "It would be lovely to take to the floor with him."

"I'm too young to dance, but I do not care," Jessamyn commented. "I can listen to the music, and I can eat! And I'm to wear a brand-new gown made of sky-blue *peau de soie*, with a necklace of pearls. Mamma got me the dearest kid gloves with pearl buttons, and sweet slippers that match my dress. What will you be wear—"

Abruptly, she stopped speaking when she saw the look of stricken realization on my face.

This whole thing had been just a cruel game of my stepmother's.

My spirits plunged as deep as they had risen only moments before. "I haven't a stitch to my name that isn't made of burlap," I said. Soon after Wilhemina had moved into Lancastyr Manor, all my beautiful clothing had somehow disappeared.

"But surely you may borrow one of Eustacia's gowns?" Jessamyn said. "She has so many."

I shook my head. "Can you imagine what she would say to that? Besides, her frocks wouldn't fit me. No, dear one," I said over a sigh. "I'll stay home. It doesn't matter."

This was untrue, and we both knew it.

Just then the curtain was pushed aside by a shaky, veined hand, and my father stepped into the nook.

"Hello, little ladies," he said with a vague smile. He wore no wig today, and his gray hair was spiky, as if he'd been running his fingers through it at random. "How nice to hear such pleasant voices coming from the window seat!"

I stood up. He seemed much like his old self. Perhaps...

"Yes, Papa!" I heard my own desperate eagerness and winced inside. "We're excited about the upcoming ball at the royal palace. May I have a new dress to wear for it?"

"Of course, sweet girl, of course." He patted my head. "Anything you desire. Did I not already consent to the purchase of several ball gowns? But I suppose you must have something special to dazzle the prince, and have it you shall. Dear me! How extravagant we have become."

I turned quickly to Jessamyn, who was watching, wide-eyed. "Did you hear that, Sister? Papa says I may have a gown made up! Will you bear witness in front of my stepmother? Why, what is wrong? Why do you look at me so?"

"Rose," Jessamyn said quietly, "perhaps you are forgetting something."

"Yes?"

"The ball is tomorrow."

A ball gown takes months to make up. The fittings, the assembly and stitching, the refittings, the embellishment, the nips and the tucks, the turnings and hems.

I clutched at my stomach, glad for once that it was empty.

"Young lady, are you quite well?" my father asked with courtly politeness. He had forgotten again who I was.

After a brief struggle, I mastered myself. I dropped a kiss on his withered cheek and smoothed his hair. "Oh, yes, yes. I am excellent, thank you, Papa. And Jessamyn, you're quite right. Silly me, thinking to have a dress made up in one day. I apologize. Now, if you will excuse me, Papa, Sister . . ."

I curtsied to them both, snatched a candle from the window ledge, and ran up to the attic. When I reached my dark room, seared by humiliation and fury and helplessness, I shoved the candle into a crude wooden holder and dropped onto the cot in a hunched position. I felt my shoulders shake, but I would not give my stepmother the victory of making me cry now. I took deep, shuddering breaths, reaching for calm.

Some moments passed before I realized the thin blanket underneath me felt lumpier and somehow softer than usual. I squinted at it curiously in the low glow of the candle.

Then I leapt off the cot, amazed.

Covering the meager bedding was a magnificent gown of costly cloth-of-gold, beside an undergarment of fine white silk, all in the style of the last century. I turned my head and saw there was a fancy farthingale beside the window, and a white neck ruff arranged neatly beside my pillow, as though the long-ago Queen Lizbeth of Nance herself had emerged from the pages of history books, taken off her finery, and left it behind.

What on earth?

I cast a wild glance about, hoping to catch a clue as to what this might possibly mean.

And then I saw them.

There, standing just a few feet away from me in the weak candlelight, were Blackie and Frump-Bum.

"You!" I gasped.

They were not alone. There was another large rat with them, a sleek white one who had a distinctly female, almost regal, air about her, and fifty—no, a hundred—no, what looked like a veritable *host* of mice waiting there, too.

Incomprehension gave way to a strange dread. I groped for the sapphire ring in my bodice, and held it tight as if to ward off evil. My entire body was shaking.

"You—Blackie—" I stammered. "How can this be?"

He stood mute, looking at me.

Wheels and gears turned in my head, spun, caught, spun again. "Am I to understand that you brought this clothing here, as you have brought me food before? But how did you know I needed it? And how did you carry it? You would all have had to work together . . . It's just not possible."

Blackie's gaze was dark and locked with mine.

He was only a beast, a lowly beast. How could he have aught to do with a ball gown?

Silence within, silence without. And many little

furry animals, watching me as if they expected I would eventually understand.

"What are you?" I blurted, as though they could answer. "What manner of person or power has sent you?" Feeling the first stirrings of terror, I backed away toward the door, step by careful step.

Then Blackie turned to Frump-Bum and made a low series of sounds.

As if on command, Frump-Bum scurried to a corner of the room and began to push a red leather book across the dusty floor with his shoulder and snout. Efficiently, purposefully, he brought it toward me, as though he did this sort of thing every day. Then he dropped back on his haunches and looked up into my astonished face.

Blackie made more commanding noises, this time aimed in my direction. Though I am not a rat, I could recognize the tone of authority when I heard it. I was being told to do something.

Still trembling, clutching my family's ring in my left hand, I moved forward and leaned over. With my right hand, I picked up the book. It was very old, and gave off a slight smell of mildew. I could just make out the words stamped in gold across the cover: *Baron Dominick de Lancastyr, Sherriff of Lancashyrre, Knight of the Sacred Order of the Tyne, Keeper of the Privy Seal and Lord of the Anglander March. His Book.*

I almost dropped it.

"Baron Dominick was the first Lancastyr!" I said, looking at Blackie. "My ancestor. Why, this book must be over two hundred years old!"

The black rat—a pet to me, a menace to most—held my astonished gaze and ever so slowly, ever so deliberately, nodded his smooth head.

Too much.

I fainted, crumpling into a heap on the bare boards of the floor.

An agitated chorus of twitters and *ack ack ack* sounds awakened me. Something was swarming across my body. With a cry, I brushed at my torso, making frantic, sweeping slaps. My hands met tiny warm balls of fur and sent them flying in every direction as they emitted squeaks of distress.

Mice! They'd been crawling all over me! Good Lord's hooks, what were they doing? Were they going to eat me alive?

When I shot up to a sitting position, I saw fat wax candles positioned in each corner of the room, making it as bright as day. And . . . o' Lord, o' Lord . . . I was wearing the Queen Lizbeth gown.

The mice now huddled in a corner at a safe distance, chattering faintly, watching my every move as if in fear. In their tiny paws I saw the gleam of silvery needles, trailing golden thread.

I felt that I had lost my reason. I would be carted off to the madhouse, and the Lancastyrs would be no more.

But before I could give way to utter panic, I felt a warm, comforting weight curl up in my lap. Catching my breath, I looked down and saw Blackie. I hugged him to me and buried my face against his fur. He smelled clean and sweet, like lavender and lemon water. Do rats bathe? This rat must have.

"Oh, Blackie!" I exclaimed.

He poked his snout into my cheek and nuzzled me a bit, until my head cleared and the worst of my fears subsided.

"Did you and the mice dress me in this gown?" I inquired at last in a whisper, as if someone might overhear. "Did you somehow find out about the ball, and you gave me this . . . this marvelous gift, just as you gave me the ring before?"

He nodded again. I felt the nod, rather than saw it,

because his face was still against mine. "Do you understand me?" I asked.

Another nod. I was not mad; my tame rat understood human speech.

"Blackie, how can this be?"

He nimbly hopped from my lap and went to the red book my ancestor had written. He ruffled through the pages until he came to a particular one and pointed to it. Then he looked at me as if to say, *Well, come on, then.*

I snatched up the book and focused on the passage Blackie had indicated. It was difficult to make out the quaint old language and the odd spelling of my ancestor, yet I was able to understand it after some moments' struggle.

Kin of our kin, this captaine of the shippe upon which our ancestors arrived at this lande, Captaine Ulum by name, when he was given to understande that by the effort of the rats alone was his vessel saved from sinking, for, lowly creetures tho' they be, they had filled the breeche in the hold with sackes of grain, thusly preventing the seas from rushing in to overwhelme the shippe…When Ulum, then, understoode this miracle, then swore he, ne'er shall there be strife between rat and any descendant of mine, as long as there be sun in skye and man on terra firma; yea, said he, tho' rats be the most despised of creatures, ne'er shall my son nor my son's sons so despise them; and none shall slaye them in shippe or house, unto the sun's darkeninge at the breaking of the Seventh Seal at the end of days.

Prince Char

I could see Rose's mind working.

"No one in my family has knowledge of this book," she said, her eyes bigger and rounder than ever.

"Because in order to protect it from one of your brainless great-grandfathers, who remodeled the library and let his decorators burn thousands of precious volumes, we stole it and hoarded it in our treasure chamber for about one hundred years," I replied in my own language. "Though it was forgotten by the Lancastyrs, that book is our charter. It gives the details of a pact between an ancient goddess, your family, and my people. This agreement is what gave the rats on Captain Ulum's ship—and their descendants—long life and intelligence far above that of ordinary rat-folk. The book tells us that if the line of the Lancastyrs should ever come to an end, we rats will return to what we once were."

She didn't need to understand me. She could fill in the blanks for herself. At last, we had broken the long silence between humans and rats, and the charter had been shared with the Lancastyrs once more. I had done it.

I, Prince Char.

Rose's jewel-like eyes closed. "Ah," she said. "A mystery is solved. The Lancastyr coat of arms features a sable rat, to the right side of a ship, under crossed swords. My father told me it was a device indicating persistence, endurance, cleverness. The rat may indeed have represented those qualities, but clearly the device tells the tale of our ancestor Captain Ulum and the rats." Then she looked at me.

I nodded again. The coat of arms she mentioned was the same one etched upon the ring I had given her.

"Where did you get this gown?" she asked.

Millennia of history before her—a family tale dating from the time of the Phoenicians—yet her first question was about a dress?

Nonetheless I would have explained, had I had

the power of human speech. I would have taken her to our storerooms and treasure troves to reveal that over the centuries, we rats had secretly saved a magnificent garment from the wardrobe of each Lady Lancastyr whose elegance we had particularly admired.

But I could communicate none of this to her. And it was more important that she read the entire book her ancestor wrote, so I slapped it with one paw.

"Yes, you gave me a magnificent present. Thank you from the bottom of my heart!" she gushed, not understanding. "I will read it when I have time, after the ball. And I cannot ever properly express my gratitude to you for the gown!"

Realizing I had done everything I could to draw her attention to the book, I looked over at Swiss and sighed. Then I stood up tall and swept Lady Rose a low, courtly bow. As I placed a paw upon my chest and brought my whiskers toward the floor, I hoped it would convey what I wished I could say aloud: *The dress is my royal gift to you, Lady Rose.*

"Oh, God save!" she cried. I could tell my action was so unexpected to her as to be frightening.

However, she calmed herself in an instant. Then her green eyes held mine as she favored me with the magnificent curtsy she'd given her stepmother the day before. This time, the move was as solemn as it was graceful.

"Thank you, Blackie," she murmured while she sank to the ground amid waves of golden skirts. "You and your people, and the mice, honor me greatly. I am proud to wear the gift of the rats, protectors of my family."

My mother and Swiss, who'd remained at the margins of these events, now came forward to stand next to me.

"She may be human," Lady Apricot said, breathing in the girl's scent curiously. "But there is something about her. She has the air of a queen, indeed. I now see why the humans have always thought her beautiful."

"My apologies, but I don't think I will ever find her beautiful," said Swiss. "She does smell extremely toothsome, though. Like sugarplums. She's lucky we're civilized enough not to bite her cheeks as she sleeps."

"If she were a rat, she would be called Lady Sugarplum," I declared.

Lady Apricot gave a most unladylike "Humpf!"

80

The day of the ball dawned fair and clear.

I awoke that morning with fierce exhilaration burning in my breast. My bid to put Lady Rose at the side of the next king would be a gamble with little risk to us rats and an enormous payoff if we succeeded. Indeed, in light of the latest developments, luck seemed to be on our side. The mice had worked long into the night to put the final touches on Rose's impressive garment, fashioned to thwart Wilhemina's mean-spirited plan. They had discarded the outmoded ruff and large farthingale and changed the shape of the billowing skirts and narrow bodice. The rat-candidate for queen would attend the party and be in line for the human throne before the evening was out.

Oh, the bliss and confidence of ignorance.

"Mother," I said over the remnants of our breakfast—fresh eggs stolen from the henhouse, shreds of venison, and day-old bread scattered across a single gold plate on the floor of my chamber—"did you match Lady Rose's garments with adornments from our treasure boxes?"

"Indeed I did."

"Thank you. When you deliver them, don't wake her up if she's still asleep. She needs her rest."

"As you wish, Your Highness," she replied in a

resentful tone, but with a regal inclination of her head. Then she added, "When you reach Castle Wendyn, thieve something pretty for me."

"My lady," I admonished, "great deeds are afoot. This is not about you and your jewel box."

"I know very well who this is about," she said, and turned her back.

My, but she seems moody today, I thought. I judged it wisest to make no comment.

Instead I proceeded with Swiss to the throne room, where my elite team of rat-warriors was waiting to start our expedition to Castle Wendyn. As you may recall, there were five of them: Corncob, a stout older rat with street experience; Truffle, a lean and dangerous black-furred female with extra-sharp teeth; and a trio of brave brown brothers, Beef One, Beef Two, and Beef Three, whom no one could tell apart. They each wore strips of jerked, dried meat around their necks, as is customary for soldiers departing on a long march. Their eager faces, their paws curled like claws, and their anticipatory chatter showed they were prepared for any sort of perilous deeds.

Yet, I'd stretched the truth a bit about needing a stalwart force in order to venture across the city.

In fact, I had almost lied.

Because there is no danger at all involved in the trip, unless you count snaking through drainpipes and swimming in sewers to be dangerous. If you're human, it might well be so. If you're a rat, it's a little pleasant exercise. As for the oh-so-fearsome Southern Rat Realm, their princess, Mozzarella, was once daring and dauntless but had become extremely lazy since ascending the throne. She probably would not care a whit whether we passed through her domain or not.

To be completely honest (and I always am, unless it is not to the purpose), during my earlier appearance in the throne room I'd played up the drama of the moment to give my people the pleasure of being witnesses and participants in a great endeavor.

That is how rats get the chance to feel like heroes. It's also how princes get featured in songs and stories.

"Brave citizens of my realm!" I now shouted to the group of five.

They pointed their snouts in my direction, inhaling my scent of excitement and determination.

"We shall reconnoiter the royal castle and find Prince Geoffrey; then we will remain to spy upon him. I am in the lead with Royal Councillor Swiss. You bring up the rear, my loyal subjects, and in case of attack, fight tooth, fight nail, fight to the death!"

Swiss's snort was drowned out by a shrill battle cry arising from five rat-throats, and off we charged.

It took over an hour to get to Castle Wendyn. I hesitate to describe our route in detail, for I do not wish to provide any interfering humans with the means to block rat access points. Suffice it to say, we began by sliding into a hole in the carved wooden pipe beneath a particular, unspecified sink at Lancastyr Manor. (Even the largest rat, my friends, can squeeze into an opening no wider than a walnut.) This led us to the public pipeline of hollowed tree trunks under the street, and from there to the large, rushing stone sewers.

We stood together on the cobbled bank of the fast-moving, rank-smelling underground river, eyeing it with distaste. "In we go!" I declared.

"Must we?" Swiss complained. "Surely we could run alongside it. The ledge is wide enough."

The other rats looked at him, shocked, as if he'd

just admitted to cowardice. Beefs One, Two, and Three made rather rude noises.

Then the ferocious Truffle stood tall on her haunches, gave Swiss a disparaging glance, and said, "If Prince Char so orders, I shall swim through the filthiest sewer water and run through fire to fulfill our mission."

I smiled at Swiss's annoyed expression before cautioning the others, "My brave followers, do not forget that in the contest for rulership that made me prince, Royal Councillor Swiss came in second, and his courage is unquestioned. This moment is an example of how he wisely protects us. He would never tell us to undergo a hardship—such as swimming this foul current—unless it were absolutely necessary. But, Swiss," I said to him, "we must go by water, for it is faster by far than we can run."

"Thank you for reminding this company of my prowess, Your Highness," Swiss said with dignity, while the others had the grace to look ashamed. "There may in fact be another alternative to swimming. Warriors, look about for something to use as a raft."

After some nosing around, Corncob found an old wine crate that had gotten caught up in a clumped eddy of straw and refuse. Swiss held on to one of the wooden slats with his tail as the rest of us piled in; then he pushed it into the current and took a flying jump to land inside.

We were off, at a spanking pace.

"Nice, eh?" Swiss said, and grinned at me.

"Heroically uncomfortable," I replied as I watched my warriors scramble about with every roll of the leaky wooden craft.

We knew we had reached Castle Wendyn when we caught sight of a stairway carved with the seal of the human royal family of Angland. We leapt off our crate and swam over to the steps, ran up them single file, and emerged in the palace dungeons.

"Don't bother to dry yourselves," I announced in a low tone. "We must find a source of clean water and wash in it. All the stealth in the world will do us no good if our stench betrays our presence to the humans."

As things turned out, the most hazardous part of our inbound mission was the washing up. When we located a pail of water by a set of stone stairs leading up and out of the dungeons, we plunged ourselves into it one by one to get the task done. Just as the last of us was finishing, we heard the approach of a palace guard. The situation would still have been fine had not Truffle, in her haste to quit the wooden bucket, knocked it to the stone floor with a loud clunk.

"Hey!" the guard shouted, rounding the corner and chasing us. "Dirty, disgusting creatures. I'll chop off your tails!"

Greatness is often misunderstood in this world.

Truffle apologized while we squeezed safely inside a narrow crack in the stone wall. I turned to her with reassuring words on the tip of my tongue. However, before I could utter them, the voice of a strange rat came from behind us.

"What is your mission here, visitors to the Southern Rat Realm?"

Royal sigh. I had hoped to do this swiftly, in and out, with no inconvenient encounters with Princess Mozzarella or her people. I pushed forward to face the owner of the voice, a gnarled little gray rat with extremely large eyes.

"Hail, Southern Realmer," I said. "I am Prince Char of the Northern Rat Realm."

He appeared duly impressed and bowed and twittered a bit.

I calmed him down by saying, "We wish to pay a

visit to Her Highness, Princess Mozzarella." I gave Swiss a look that warned him not to comment upon this blatant falsehood. Then I smiled at the gray rat. "Will you lead us to her?"

He gave an excited bounce and replied, "With pleasure!"

We followed our guide through a convoluted series of burrowed passages into a dark throne room of such squalor, such disarray, you would not believe me if I tried to describe it in detail. The last time I'd visited Mozzarella was many years before, and the place had been a sty even then. Now it was almost impassable, with droppings, dry bones in piles, and dust everywhere.

The Southern Realmers lived in the royal castle of the humans, and this was the best they could achieve?

"Why, if it isn't the handsome Prince Char!"

The luscious, languid voice came from a black rat so enormously plump, you would surely have taken her for a woodchuck had you encountered her in the dark. Yet I doubted whether anyone would ever encounter her anywhere but in the throne room itself these days, for I could not imagine how she was able to move with so much bulk around her middle.

She was surrounded by various courtiers in similar states of poundage.

"At least we need not fear a swift attack," Swiss whispered.

"Please forgive me if I don't rise to greet you," Mozzarella apologized. "I have had a bit of trouble with that lately, Your Highness. What brings you here?"

"My brave companions and I are on a quest to discover whatever we may about the succession to the human throne. We wish to eavesdrop on Good King Tumtry and his son, Geoffrey."

"Good heavens, why?" She widened her dark eyes at me. "What could they possibly say that would be of interest?"

Swiss and the five warriors murmured at this. But the princess meant no disrespect; she was just too self-absorbed to care for anything but her own indulgence. I silenced them with a wave of my tail. "Princess Mozzarella, I only wish to determine whether the son of Good King Tumtry is fit to rule. Have you heard any tattle about it?"

"Dear, dear Prince Char, I have no concern about the affairs of humans. None whatsoever. Yet I grant you safe conduct through my realm, to do whatever you wish, as long as you don't take any loot."

"That is just and kind," I said with a bow.

Mozzarella heaved a sigh. "Ah, Prince Char, you are so very dashing. Are you sure you did not come hither to court me, and reunite the Northern and Southern Rat Realms under one banner?"

I avoided looking at Swiss. "Alas, dear Princess," I said in the smoothest voice I could manage, "I am already pledged to another."

What? How had those words come out of my mouth? And why did the image of Rose de Lancastyr come to mind when I said them?

"You are not!" Swiss said in a low, low voice.

"It's the only way to get out of this without offending her," I whispered.

He grumbled, "This is how gossip starts."

After further exchanges of pleasantries and some stupendous snacks, Mozzarella at last sent us off to seek Prince Geoffrey in the largest ballroom, where tonight's event was no doubt taking place. Once again, we had the little gray rat to guide us.

CINDERELLA

The day of the ball had arrived and, with it, a thousand chores.

"Cinderella!" Cook shouted from the scullery. "Where is that egg-white mask for the mistress? Pye tells me her maid is still waiting for it!"

"Almost ready! I have only to add the crushed strawberries." My stomach gurgled with hunger as I vigorously whisked the eggs in a wooden basin. I knew my stepmother would be asking next for cucumber slices to lay upon her eyelids so as to reduce their puffiness, and goose-fat salve for her dry hands. I would gladly have eaten what Wilhemina was about to put on her skin, but fine foods like cucumbers and strawberries were not wasted on menials like myself.

The entire household belowstairs had been toiling for hours to help prepare for the upcoming extravaganza, in addition to our regular tasks. As there were so few of us, the load was heavy.

Yet my spirits were light. For while I labored, I wondered at the miraculous events of the night before. The rats, the mice, the gown... And to add marvel upon marvel, this morning the pretty, feminine white rat had awoken me by dropping a necklace of huge square emeralds on the floor by my cot. No doubt, the ornate (if rather dirty) piece of jewelry had been stolen long ago from another Lancastyr ancestor.

This evening I would escape my imprisonment, if only for one night. And who knew what I might accomplish?

I mixed the smashed strawberries into the beaten egg whites and poured the whole into a small silver creamer. I then rushed it over to the lady's maid, who stood impatiently tapping her foot outside the kitchen's arched doorway. She would never enter the realm where food was prepared; she considered it beneath her. She snatched the creamer from me without a word of thanks and flounced away to attend to her mistress.

"As snooty as a duchess, that one," Pye remarked, passing by with a broom.

I smiled at him as we went back into the kitchen.

Unfortunately, at this moment Cook emerged from the scullery carrying a copper pot. She didn't like it when I smiled. "What do you have to smirk at, lazy wench? Miss Jessamyn needs you in her bedchamber. Go quick. Here, you, boy!" she yelled to Pye. "Make the luncheon trays ready for the family. Remember, Miss Eustacia can't abide watercress, Lord Lancastyr gets no soup, for he might spill, and Lady Wilhemina gets the dish of mustard with her sliced ham."

Pye always had trouble remembering which dishes went on which tray—and his preparations inevitably ended in scoldings and tears. He threw me a beseeching glance.

I rushed to aid him. "Oh, Cook, please allow me to arrange the trays for you before I go upstairs," I said. "It will take but a moment."

"Don't you argue with my orders, girl! If I say the boy does the trays, he does the trays. Now step lively and see to Miss Jessamyn."

I nodded, while Pye put down his broom and moved to obey with an air of resignation.

I hastened to Jessamyn's suite.

"Dear Sister!" She stuck her small head out her bedchamber door as I drew near. "Hurry!"

I followed her inside and gave her a hug.

"I've been waiting for you," she said, wiggling with nervousness as soon as I released her. "I worked through the whole night on a plan to bring you to the ball with us."

My conscience pricked me. "You shouldn't have! What is it, darling?"

"Look." She led me to her pink-and-cream dressing room. There upon a small sofa lay one of her own gowns. She had unpicked the hem of the skirt so that it was a full two inches longer than it had been before. "What do you think?" Jessamyn asked. "I did it myself. Could you wear it? I am just a little girl, but I am quite chubby, and you have become so thin that perhaps it would do. Oh, try it on, do try it on!"

A lump rose in my throat, but I managed to say at last, "You are a gentle and generous child."

I knew just by looking that it would not fit, but she had labored upon the garment with such love that I agreed to try it. And, as I thought, I could not ease it down over my bosom, nor would it rise past my hips when I attempted to step in and pull it up.

"Oh, Rose!" Jessamyn began to cry.

I felt awash in guilt. I almost broke down and confessed everything that had taken place with the rats the night before, but I worried that in her excitement, she might slip and reveal the secret to her mother.

Thank goodness, at that moment Pye appeared at Jessamyn's doorway with her luncheon tray. I accepted it on her behalf and tried to cheer her with tea and sandwiches. After a while I was able to convince her to eat a few bites; then I fairly flew back to the kitchen.

"So your fine ladyship at last decides to join us!" Cook snarled at me. "It's past time for you to give Miss Eustacia her milk bath. The buckets are over there in the corner, fresh and warm from the cow. Hop along! And when you're finished, Lady Wilhemina wants you to brush her hair."

Oh, lovely. My favorite task.

I hauled bucket after bucket upstairs to fill the deep, shell-shaped bathtub in Eustacia's sunny bathroom, which had once been mine. With my mother, on a long-ago visit to the Anglish coast, I had collected the starfish and scallop shells that still lay scattered across the lip of the tub. In some ways, it was easier for me to live in the attic than it would have been to dwell in these family chambers, haunted by the ghosts of a happy childhood.

"Faster, Cinderella, you laggard!" Eustacia stood by in a ruffled white satin wrapper and poufy feathered slippers with an impatient frown on her red face. "I must be ready soon, and you are late, late, late! I shall tell Mamma."

"As you wish," I replied serenely.

Oh, how she despised it when I was serene. "You . . . you . . ." she sputtered.

"Yes?" I smiled at her.

She stared at me for a moment, then her gaze faltered and she looked down at the floor with a sullen pout. "Nothing."

When the milk had been poured and sweet-smelling oils added, she settled into the bath. I did my best to scrub away the pink blemishes on her back with a sponge.

"Ow!" she exclaimed. "What are you doing?" She pinched the soft underflesh of my arm.

"I'm handling you as gently as a newborn puppy, Eustacia."

"Are you comparing me to a dog?" She slapped away my wet fingers, grabbed the sponge, and threw it at me. "Get out!"

For once, I was glad to do her bidding. But my next duty required me to enter Wilhemina's chambers, which had once belonged to my mother. It was almost unbearable to pass through the gaily flower-painted doors, only to see my stepmother seated at my mother's vanity table, awaiting me with her cold gaze.

Without a sound, she handed me her silver-backed hairbrush. I took it, careful not to touch her during the transfer, and proceeded to brush her hair one hundred strokes. To keep myself from remembering how my mother and I used to arrange each other's hair in such a different spirit, one of lightness and love, I once again revisited in my thoughts the scene that had taken place in my attic room the night before.

I recalled the brilliant eyes of Blackie. The knightly bow he'd executed with such bizarre grace.

"Dreaming of the ball, girl? Keep your mind on your work," Wilhemina said. "Woe betide you if my tresses are not perfect when you finish."

I forced my attention to the task.

Prince Char

Twisting and turning, the little gray rat led our venturesome band through a labyrinth of ancient, dusty tunnels in the walls of Castle Wendyn.

We passed many scattered trinkets and interesting bits of loot. Beef Two (at least I think it was Beef Two, though it might have been Beef Three or even Beef One) picked up a silver bracelet that hung from a splinter and was about to slip it over his head.

"Drop it," Swiss ordered. "Didn't you listen to Princess Mozzarella? We are not to take anything from the Southern Rat Realm."

Shamefaced, the Beef brother hung it back upon the splinter. His siblings yelled at him about the family honor as we continued on.

The Southern Realmers we passed seemed an undisciplined lot. They nibbled food as they moved along, and gave us no civil greetings. One of them even winked rudely at Truffle, who responded by looming over him with such a powerful frown that the fellow slunk away in embarrassment.

"I wouldn't stand for this in my own realm, not for one moment," I said to Swiss in a disgusted aside.

When at last we arrived at a crawl space in the ceiling just above the ballroom, I peered through a crack to assess the situation. Then I whispered to my valiant companions, "My warriors, there is a man with a huge crown upon his head sitting upon a throne directly below us."

"King Tumtry!" our guide exclaimed. "May I have a look?"

I gave him room and he observed for a moment. "Yes, it is indeed the king. However, Your Highness, I regret that I see no sign of Prince Geoffrey. He has long golden hair and usually wears a small crown."

"Then we will have to watch and wait for him," I declared. "Now listen, everyone, there's an enormous chandelier beneath us—in fact, it is right below where Corncob is standing." I pointed with my tail. "Thank heavens the candles are not yet lit for the ball. If

Swiss and I could only get down there and hide among the crystals, we could hear and see everything."

"Good plan, Your Highness!" one of the Beef brothers cried, then ducked as his siblings pushed him and told him to be quiet and speak only when spoken to.

I ignored them and moved over to Corncob, who bowed and shuffled aside as I approached. "Aha," I said, nosing about the hole where the chandelier's hook was attached to the boards. "There is a small point of entry here. Swiss and I will make our way through it while you remain behind to keep our escape route clear."

"We shall fight off all comers!" Truffle cried. "No one will interfere with Prince Char's great mission!"

"Hooray!" shouted the others. The gray guide rat joined in with enthusiasm.

"Ssshhh." Swiss rounded on them and frowned. "You'll betray our position to the humans."

They quieted on the instant.

It's not easy to descend the metal hoops and volutes of a chandelier, but Swiss and I did so. We stepped and sidled and clung and crept until we were within earshot of the humans. It was a good thing there was so much bustle in the ballroom, or someone would almost certainly have noticed us.

King Tumtry, from his big silver throne, held audience after audience with tradespeople, musicians, floral designers, the majordomo, the chatelaine, and many others. He was flanked by two richly garbed noblemen, one at his right hand and one on his left. They participated in the discussions. But I saw neither hide nor hair of the prince.

"Those nobles by the king's side must be the royal councillors," Swiss observed, "just as I am yours."

We kept watch while the shiny floors—made of pink marble, set with slivers of black onyx to form a geometrical pattern—rang with the *click-clack* of many heels. Irksome discussions of the number of guests and the appropriateness of the music and the potential for rainy weather went round and round in our heads. My interest was briefly caught when the chief cook bowed to the king and gave an account of the various dainties that would be served at the feast (including pear tarts stuffed with gorgonzola and pecans), but when he left, I felt disappointment and rising impatience. The hands of the big clock in the gallery ticked by the hours, until it was three o'clock.

"Don't you think we should seek Cinderella's prince somewhere else?" Swiss hissed at me.

"No, we stay," I decided. "This is the center of the action. He must turn up here sooner or later."

As more minutes passed, I felt the chandelier begin to tip. Alarmed, I looked over to see that my royal councillor had fallen asleep and was leaning precariously sideways.

"Swiss!" I snapped.

"Huh?"

"Pay attention!"

Yet another hour dragged by. When the room was finally empty of everyone except King Tumtry and his two councillors (and by this time, I was actually beginning to question my own orders), our persistence at last yielded a result. I caught a few words, spoken by the king in an undertone. "Geoffrey ... not sure ... I think ... "

Aha!

I inched closer, concerned that if I did not use infinite care, all the blasted pretty, moving, twinkling bits and bobs of the chandelier would call attention to me.

The life of a rat is fraught with such moments.

"Your Majesty," said one of the councillors, a big

man with a large brown beard and a pointy-tipped mustache, "please do not fall victim to your fears. This ball is the very best idea we have yet hit upon. We must allow it to take place."

"Lord Hamp, it is not fear, but my conscience that troubles me," the king replied.

The other courtier, tall and thin with lank gray hair and a worried expression, looked suddenly even more worried. "Your Majesty, I would like to agree with Lord Hamp, but are you *sure* your son can maintain his, er, peace for the length of the night—dancing, mingling with guests until dawn, making polite conversation?"

The king looked old and drawn. His chin, veiled by a white wisp of beard, was sunken into the purple velvet of his royal robe, and while I watched, he took off his ermine-trimmed crown and set it upon his lap. I sniffed hard in his direction and caught a scent of inutterable weariness, with a strong note of despair. The same despair came through in his voice. "Lord Brimfield, Geoffrey must do this," he said. "The fate of my kingdom depends on it. May heaven and the spirit of my dear departed wife, Monette, send us salvation tonight. May there be a decent, intelligent lady here whom my son will wed."

Lord Brimfield said, "The prince laughed at me this morning and told me he will marry only if we bring him the fairest woman ever born."

"That is not the nobility of spirit with which my queen and I tried to raise our son," the king said. "Yet if what he told you is indeed so, there is hope, Brimfield!"

"I beg your pardon—what does Your Majesty mean?"

"If memory serves—if my old age is not playing tricks upon me," King Tumtry wheezed, "we may very well bring Geoffrey what he requires. Did you send an invitation to Lancastyr Manor? Lord Lancastyr has a daughter . . ."

"We did, Your Majesty." Lord Hamp inclined his head and fingered a jeweled orb that hung from his neck on a long gold chain. "As you commanded, we invited all Glassevale families with eligible daughters to this event. Even the Lancastyrs, though poor Lord Lancastyr has become weak in his mind and has married a woman of doubtful moral character."

"What a pity," said Lord Brimfield, "to see the Lancastyr line, so important in the history of our great country and so loyal to the throne, deteriorate into madness and possibly even ruin."

I felt anger at this characterization of our special humans.

The fact that it was true only made it worse.

"But, you fools," thundered King Tumtry, "have you never seen the Lancastyr daughter?"

You may be sure I was all attention at this juncture.

Lord Hamp seemed taken aback. "Sire, she is a most ill-favored, frownsome wench. Not at all to the purpose. She has never been to the palace, of course, but her mother thrusts her forward at every social gathering to which she may gain entrance, so I have seen her quite recently—though Barnaby de Lancastyr does not accompany her. What is the name . . . Eulalia? Anastasia?"

"Eustacia," supplied Lord Brimfield, with a faint sneer.

"Eustacia, Eustacia! Don't you 'Eustacia' me like a couple of old roosting hens!" the king shouted. "That's the stepdaughter, no doubt! I'm talking about the daughter of the late Lady Jane, the first wife of Lord Lancastyr—she who was Jane de Fribourg before marrying."

"Oh, Lady Jane the Lovely! Of course," Lord Hamp said.

Then Lord Brimfield exclaimed, "What a lackwit

I am! I have indeed heard of the Lancastyr girl. Her name is Rose, and since a special dispensation was granted to the Lancastyrs centuries ago to bestow a courtesy title to their heir, she is known as Lady Rose. She made her debut at fifteen and caused quite a stir, but no one has seen her since her father remarried."

There was silence for a moment. Then Lord Brimfield spoke again. "Now that I think upon it, I realize there was some talk about the girl's nature being so delicate, she became disordered after the death of Lady Jane—which is why she no longer goes about in society."

"Ha!" The king dismissed this idea with a curt sideways swipe of his hand. "What nonsense. It's clear that Rose de Lancastyr has fallen under the thumb of a stepmother who is jealous of her. Lancastyr Manor is evidently not a happy home. Perhaps Lady Rose would be glad to escape it . . . and that is an ideal situation for our purposes, is it not?"

Swiss whispered, "Things are looking good for the rat-candidate."

It did sound as though Prince Geoffrey would do as I'd hoped, and choose Rose because of her fine looks. But I felt stirrings of uneasiness in my chest. I did not quite understand what the king meant by "an ideal situation for our purposes."

So I paid close attention when Lord Hamp spoke once again. "Very well," he said, "since it appears the young lady may meet our needs, let us hope Rose de Lancastyr will be in attendance at the ball tonight."

I still was not enlightened. What exactly were the needs to which Hamp referred?

Suddenly, the giant double oaken doors facing the throne were flung open to admit the tall figure of a young man wearing a crown, trailed by several people who were probably a mixture of courtiers and servants. "Father! Father!" he called in a rich, musical voice—the sort of voice I thought human girls would find compelling.

King Tumtry sat upright and hastily dropped his own crown upon his head. It slid a little to one side.

Meanwhile, I took stock of the famous Prince Geoffrey.

"Ooooh, he's so haaaaandsome," Swiss cooed.

Swiss was teasing, of course, but according to what I knew of humans, I believed the shining Geoffrey should please Rose greatly, at least in the matter of looks.

So why was I not pleased?

"Yes, my son?" King Tumtry asked, blinking a little as Geoffrey rapidly advanced toward the throne.

"Father, this knavish fool has endangered the success of tonight's ball before it has even begun!" The prince flung an accusing finger toward a bowing, scraping man who, with his thick lips and balding head, seemed quite as harmless as he was frightened. The prince's eyes were fierce, and his golden hair moved as he did, dramatically.

"Come now, Son," King Tumtry said. "Let the man explain. What is your name, my good fellow?"

"Quintilius Porter, Your Majesty," he said, and exhaled heavily as he got down upon one knee before the throne. "I was charged with delivering and installing the great artist Fieresci's marble statue of your son, His Royal Highness, in time for tonight's ball. I was to install it in the center of the Fountain of Love in the courtyard, to bring good fortune to the prince as he chooses his bride."

"And instead, what do you think he has done?" Geoffrey bellowed. "The clumsy oaf has allowed one of the arms to break off!"

"That certainly sounds unfortunate," the king said carefully. "Yet perhaps all is not lost. What think you, my lord councillors?"

"Master Porter," said Lord Hamp, "can the statue be mended by tonight?"

"Oh yes, yes, Lord Hamp, we can reattach the arm with a strong bolt, and then—if I may be so bold as to make the suggestion—I should drape a velvet cloak across the shoulders of the statue to hide the break. After the ball, the sculptor will be able to do a more thorough job of repairing his work." Quintilius Porter did not raise his eyes. "I exceedingly regret the carelessness of my assistants. I humbly beg your pardon, Your Majesty. I will remain at the ball tonight if you wish, out of sight, with the sole object of watching over the statue."

Lord Hamp gave a guarded smile. "Your Majesty, so long as Master Porter makes good on his promise, His Highness the prince need have no fear. He shall laugh and dance the night away with many a beautiful woman, secure in the knowledge that he has been blessed with good fortune by the statue in the fountain."

"I will do so, Lord Hamp," said Geoffrey, drawing his sword and turning to Quintilius Porter. "But this lout shall not be in attendance."

He raised the blade high in both hands. Then he swung it down hard, striking off the unsuspecting Master Porter's head.

For an instant, the world seemed suspended. I could not think or even breathe.

"Your Highness!" Swiss's cry sounded like a gurgle.

I did not reply. My attention was still riveted upon the disembodied head of Quintilius Porter, as were the gazes of all the humans in the ballroom below. The people stood frozen.

"Prince Geoffrey is evil—or mad!" Swiss cried, more coherently now, but quite unnecessarily.

I glanced across the chandelier at him. When I looked at his twirling whiskers and swiftly rotating ears, all I could see instead was Rose's kind, innocent face. Slowly, as if in the midst of a fever dream from which I could not awaken, I said: "What have I done? By the great Prince Feast, what have I done?"

Everything made sense now. Why else would a handsome crown prince like Geoffrey require such unusual measures to obtain a bride? I had assumed the issue to be that Geoffrey was difficult to please. How wrong I'd been. Doubtless, good King Tumtry had not matched his son with a foreign princess or a highborn lady of his own kingdom because such a girl could not be expected to remain married to Geoffrey once she learned he was dangerous. No, the king needed a bride for his son who was attractive yet utterly powerless, without a strong family behind her to provide refuge and support. Someone who would stay with Geoffrey because she had nowhere else to go.

Someone like Rose.

This was the "purpose" of which the king and his councillors had spoken.

What a lackwit I had been.

Swiss's hold on his perch looked unstable. "You were right, my prince! We have much to worry us in the human succession. If this vicious fellow inherits the throne, no one in Angland will be safe."

Least of all, the lady unlucky enough to become Geoffrey's wife.

"Lady Rose!" I turned tail and jumped from tier to tier of the chandelier, uncaring that I might be seen, heedless of my own safety or that of Swiss. For our dear Rose would soon be leaving Lancastyr Manor to come meet Geoffrey.

She must be stopped.

"Look!" someone shouted below us. "The spirit of the dead man rises to the ceiling! The crystals of the chandelier shake!"

This seemed to jerk the humans from their frozen positions, and pandemonium ensued.

Lord Hamp's bass voice sounded above the panic: "Bar the doors! No one departs this room until there is calm and silence! And word of this man's death must go no further!"

Swiss and I ran back to where my rat-warriors were standing guard with our guide. They had pulled off their jerked-meat collars and were sharing them around, chewing with a dull air.

"My warriors!" I yelled. "Make haste!"

They blinked at me in astonishment and dropped the jerky. They had never seen me lose my composure thus, not even for an instant.

Uncaring, I shouted even louder. "Return to Lancastyr Manor! Lady Rose's life is in danger. Away, away!"

Fur spiked, whiskers flattened, they slipped through the rafters as fast as poached eggs sliding across a polished counter.

Our gray southern guide trickled off in the opposite direction, no doubt to spread the word that Geoffrey was not the only prince who had run mad.

After we galloped for a few minutes, Swiss demanded between panting breaths, "But, Your Highness . . . is it not more important than ever . . . that Lady Rose marry the prince, to protect the kingdom from him? It is the very scenario you feared might come to pass—a bad king despoiling the land of the Food."

"When I made that suggestion, I was referring to a rat-enemy, not a lunatic," I snarled at my friend. "This Geoffrey fellow would kill our Rose within the first month! She must not go to the ball tonight!"

CINDERELLA

The evening had come at last.

Exhausted from my long list of chores, I had just finished helping Jessamyn into her blue party frock when my stepmother, clad in scarlet velvet and wearing a ruby tiara, entered the dressing chamber.

"Mamma!" Jessamyn cried, startled, for her mother seldom visited her chambers. "Whatever brings you here?"

Wilhemina ignored her. "Cinderella," she said with a wide, insincere smile as she opened a large ivory fan and fluttered it at me. Then she snapped it shut. "We must be going now. Lord Lancastyr is already waiting in the coach. What a shame you were so lazy about your tasks today; there hardly remains any time in which to ready yourself."

Biting back an angry reply, I placed a hand over my bodice, underneath which the Lancastyr ring was hidden. Strength and pride seemed to flow from it, and I squared my shoulders.

Jessamyn did not dare to speak, but she nudged herself closer to me.

Wilhemina waved her fan at my rags. "Perhaps you would like to go to your room and dress quickly, before it is too late?" she asked. "Since one cannot attend a ball wearing, shall we say, such informal attire."

I could feel her evil glee as she waited for me to tell her I had nothing to wear. Her eagerness to take joy in my misery repulsed me so much that I decided, just this once, to indulge in a wicked game of my own.

"Oh, Lady Wilhemina," I said in a trembly little voice. "Thank you for this chance. I have tried to assemble a garment from things I've found around the house ... yet I fear to shame you and my father. I do not know what you will think of it."

A grin oozed across her face. Clearly she was pondering how entertaining it would be to make me model an embarrassing homemade gown in front of her. "Very well—go put it on, silly creature. Then you may meet me and my daughters at the grand staircase. If your garb is appropriate for a royal event, I shall allow you to attend. If not, perhaps another time."

Wicked, wicked stepmother.

Jessamyn stepped forward and implored, "*Beloved* Mamma, perhaps Cinderella ought to simply remain here and take a much-needed rest tonight."

My dear sister was no doubt thinking she'd save me from humiliation this way.

"No, no." Lady Wilhemina's red lips stretched open to reveal her teeth. "A promise is a promise. If Cinderella is clad correctly, she shall come. Make haste, fool girl!" she rapped out at me. "Or we'll be departing without you."

Ha. I was certain she would not miss the coming scene of my humiliation and rejection for anything, no matter how long I delayed.

"Yes, my lady," I said, then turned on my toes to scurry upstairs.

I'd stolen the opportunity earlier to bathe in a copper tub by the kitchen fire while Cook napped, so I was clean and ready to get dressed. When I burst into my room, I saw that a group of mice and rats had assembled there to see me off, though strangely, Blackie and Frump-Bum were not among them. I stripped down to my shift, and over it I hastily donned the glorious gown the mice had crafted. After fastening all the hooks and buttons, I released my damp hair from its braids, beat at it quickly with an old brush Eustacia had discarded, and took a deep breath.

What was I forgetting?

Oh, yes. The emerald necklace.

I blew upon the jewels and did the best I could to polish them with the tepid water in the basin. Once the grime of centuries had been rubbed off, the emeralds reflected cold fire even in the weak light of my garret. I fastened the chain about my neck. Now I was ready to depart.

There was no looking glass to tell me if my efforts were successful, but when I turned around to face my rodent audience, they began to jump up and down and chirp like birds.

"Wish me good fortune!" I said to them.

They jiggled about and made more noise. It cheered me quite a bit, though I did feel keen disappointment at Blackie's absence. I thanked the rats and mice most profusely and hurried down the stairs.

One thing my rodent well-wishers had not thought of as they planned my wardrobe was shoes.

(Understandable, since they themselves had no need of such things.) Thus, beneath the elegant skirts, I was barefoot as usual. I would have to take great care as I danced at the ball so as not to shock the company by flashing my toes!

My step slowed when I came to the final flight of stairs. I switched from a rapid trot to a regal sweep. At the base of the grand staircase, arrayed in their full finery and gaping at my entrance, were my wicked stepmother and two stepsisters.

I ignored Eustacia and even Jessamyn as I floated lightly toward them, focusing entirely upon the confusion and rising fury on the face of Lady Wilhemina.

I could not help myself. After all this time of suffering under Wilhemina's yoke, I felt entitled to let triumph warm my interior.

"Oh my very goodness!" Jessamyn broke the stunned silence, her voice full of delight and awe. "Where on earth did you get that pretty, pretty gown?"

"It belonged to an ancestress," I said. "I found it in the attic."

"Well, it's simply breathtaking," she crowed. "How smitten Prince Geoffrey will be when he sees you!"

I fear this proved too much for Eustacia. A beastly howl tore from her throat.

I fell backward a step, shocked.

Never one to miss an opportunity, Wilhemina took advantage of my loss of balance by leaping forward. When I flung up an arm to ward off the expected blow, she instead reached under my elbow, hooked the long, bony fingers of both her hands into the top of my bodice, and yanked with all her might in opposite directions.

The delicate golden fabric parted with hardly a sound into two sagging pieces, which then slid off my shoulders and dropped to the marble floor.

And I stood naked but for my white muslin shift in the front hall of Lancastyr Manor.

Jessamyn gave a wail of horror. She did not stop wailing until her mother slapped her cheek. Not hard enough to raise a mark, mind you—for someone might have noticed that—but sufficient to make her daughter close her mouth and cover it with her fingers, stifling the cry she continued to make in her throat as tears streamed down her face.

Her scream had brought the few remaining servants running to the scene.

Thus it was that Mrs. Grigson, Cook, Pye,

Wilhemina's lady's maid, and the chambermaid were all treated to the spectacle my stepmother's spite and my own pride had created.

Pye ran forward to fling his tattered waistcoat across my shoulders. I could not even thank him or warn him not to bring down the wrath of my stepmother on his head. I had not the power of speech.

I was further shocked when Cook herself, who made my life a misery every day, stammered out: "Poor Cinderella—I—" Then, apparently thinking better of showing any sympathy, she snapped her mouth shut and hurried away.

"Lady Rose!" Mrs. Grigson cried out. "My dear Lady Rose!" She rushed to put her arms about me, trying to shield me with her body. "You, there, don't stand about gawking!" she shouted at the other servants. "Get back belowstairs!"

Somehow the fact that Mrs. Grigson was endangering her position here at Lancastyr Manor managed to penetrate my daze. "No, Mrs. Grigson, no—"

Her cheeks red and her eyes bright, the housekeeper brushed aside what I had been about to say. "Yes, my lady, 'tis time." She rounded on my stepmother. "You terrible woman. You've pushed until a body can stand it no longer. Torturing this innocent simply because you're jealous of her!"

Wilhemina advanced on Mrs. Grigson as if to do her a violence, but the sturdy older woman faced her down.

"I'm not like this sweet lamb, too well-mannered to strike back at a fishwife like you," the housekeeper blazed. "Go ahead. Just try to manhandle me!"

"Leave this house," my stepmother spat. "If you are not packed and gone by the time we return from the ball, I shall call the magistrates to eject you."

"Aye, ma'am, I shall go. And I'm taking Lady Rose with me."

"No!" The cry was from Jessamyn. "Do not take my sister away!"

Her mother rounded on her, grasped her shoulders, and shook her. "How dare you call her sister. Go join Lord Lancastyr in the coach, you bad, horrid child!"

I could see that Jessamyn was about to argue. This would never do. "Go, Jessamyn, dear, rest easy." My voice was dull, as hopeless as I felt. "I won't leave. You have my word upon it."

Jessamyn gave me one desperate look of sorrow tinged with relief, and pelted off down the outside staircase. Eustacia followed suit.

"My lady," Mrs. Grigson said to me while they hastened off. "Let us flee this place together."

How could I explain in front of Wilhemina that I needed to stay at Lancastyr Manor to make sure she did not murder my father? I could not burden Mrs. Grigson with that information either, for she could do nothing to help. No, it was best to let her continue thinking me a coward so that she could leave here without looking back. "My dear Mrs. Grigson... I cannot. You go, but I must remain."

The rebellious light in Mrs. Grigson's faded blue eyes went out. She was disappointed in me. I wondered why fate decreed that when I tried to be strongest, I appeared weakest.

She cried, "My lady, how could you be so spiritless? I have given up my position and my future for naught! Where is the courage and daring of your noble ancestors?" She hurried down the back stairs in a distressed flutter of gray skirts, dragging Pye with her. I hoped she would take him along when she departed; he, too, had put himself in danger by being kind to me.

Now Wilhemina burst into high, mocking laughter. Without another word, she turned a scarlet-clad shoulder and headed out to the waiting coach.

Somehow, in the next instant I found myself running down the back service passage and into the kitchen garden. There, where thick brick walls protected the rows of vegetables, I could release my grief and shame without being seen or heard. So I fell to my knees in the dirt beside a melon vine, and sobbed.

Lady Wilhemina had won. She had won, and I was alone, and the long, illustrious history of the house of Lancastyr was fated to come to a wretched end, because I had failed. There would be no catching the car of the prince or the king tonight. I would not find Sir Tompkin or Lord Bluehart.

In the lowering sunlight of the dying day, I could sense part of myself dying as well.

After the first storm of weeping, I reached into my shift pocket and tilted the comforting weight of the Lancastyr ring into my palm. I gripped it hard. "It was not too much to ask," I lamented, tasting tears on my tongue. "I wish I could go to the ball." My thumb sought the sapphire and began to rub back and forth over the Lancastyr coat of arms.

I don't know how long I grieved thus before I began to notice something happening to the Lancastyr ring. It grew cool under my fingers, when the soft gold should have warmed with the heat of my skin.

Strange, it was now giving off a wild fragrance, crisp and full of promise. What a contrast to the sluggish throb of rage and despair coursing through my veins!

I breathed in the fresh scent, feeling it revive me, as the sapphire signet continued to cool against my skin and became increasingly slippery. It moved, it wriggled. Then, in a gush, it melted into liquid. And instead of a ring there was water bubbling up in my palm, more and more of it, sparkling like fine champagne. I cupped my hands together to try to contain it, but in an instant the water brimmed over.

"Ah!" I cast it away and stood up, staring in wonder at a waterfall flowing in the air without touching the ground. The cascade hovered, shimmering with chiming laughter.

What was happening? I passed a trembling hand across my eyes.

Then the liquid took the shape of a woman who stepped down in front of me.

She glowed faintly blue, like the lavender edging our flower beds. Her thick purple-black hair fell to her ankles in lively waves. Enormous eyes, set slant-wise in her face, seemed to scatter light of their own. Now they were sapphire, now aqua, now amethyst. So dazzled was I that I cannot tell you what dress she wore—or indeed if she wore one at all.

My ring—the Lancastyr ring—had changed into this?

How?

An image of a sleek black rat popped into my head. Blackie! He'd given me the ring. This was his doing!

I would have puzzled more over it had not the woman looked at me with those changing eyes, laughed like a song, and parted her lips to speak. Oh! What wisdom of the ages would this unearthly creature grant to me, a mere mortal?

"You asked to attend this evening's ball," she said in a sweet little voice, completely unexpected in its childlike trill.

What?

She hadn't revealed the secrets of the cosmos. She'd said something else. Something about a ball. What ball?

It took all the power I could muster to speak.

"Great lady, who are you?"

She smiled, spun on tiptoe so her hair swirled around her, and said in that dulcet voice, "Do you jape at me, girl of the Lancastyrs? I adore jests and foolery! Yet your kind has always seemed so dreadfully serious to me. In fact, it's been hundreds of years since any of you have called upon me at all. What game do we play now?"

Play? I felt my jaw go slack. With great effort I gathered my wits and replied, "It is no game, my lady. I know you not. I am Rose de Lancastyr." I curtsied with as much elegance as I could in the uneven soil of the garden, worrying about my unseemly attire.

With another melting laugh, she came forward and kissed the top of my head. "You are delightful! Full of silliness," she said. "You must of course know who I am, if you summoned me. I shall grant your wish, the dearest wish of your heart. You shall attend this celebration tonight, since it is so important to you."

From the spot where she touched me, joy rippled through my body. I wanted to give way and savor this new feeling, but instead I persisted: "I don't understand. Forgive me."

"Ah."

A tiny pucker visited her perfect brow. She put a long finger to my cheek, and while bubbling lightness spread through me from that point of communion, she tilted her head sideways and studied me intently for a few moments, as if she were listening to something.

"Ah," she said again, yet it was a different sound, one of dawning comprehension, as though she'd taken possession of my thoughts through her fingertip. "I see. I understand. The ring was lost to the Lancastyrs for centuries. The rats of Lancastyr Manor stole it from your forebears. And very recently, a quite special rat has returned it!"

More laughter, and she danced away, casting her delicate wild fragrance hither and thither, stepping into the air and down to earth again.

"I know what to do, I know what to do!" she cried.

In a flash, she was before me again. I braced myself for more glorious strangeness.

"Dear Rose, also called Cinderella, I am Ashiira, your family's goddess. I have cared for your line since long before your ancestors took the name of Lancastyr, in the days of old Phoenicia. My power comes from the Great One who rules all. In antiquity, your family danced and sang for me and burned fragrant wood to please me, and in return I gave them the precious blue stone, which they could use to call upon me for aid. Yet I warned them to choose wisely before they used the stone, as I would grant their requests only once in each generation."

Did I understand aright? This goddess would grant me a wish—but only one?

"Girl of the Lancastyrs," Ashiira continued, "you have asked something of me and I shall grant your request. But this should be greatly amusing, for you have not chosen wisely! In fact, your wish was most frivolous!"

I felt my heart drop from the dizzy heights whence it had begun to climb. I hoped she did not mean what I thought she meant.

"But going to the ball was not my real wish!" I cried. "I wish to heal my father's mind, rescue my family from ruin, be rid of my stepmother, and see to it that the line of the Lancastyrs will continue unbroken."

"But that is not what you said!" she exclaimed in high glee, twinkling like a firefly. "You wished to go to the ball at Castle Wendyn tonight. And so you shall! I read the entire story in your mind just now. Let me take care of your appearance first; then we'll be off to the stable yard to see how best to convey you to the celebrations."

Before I could conceive of a way to halt the misunderstanding I had just set in motion, the fairy-goddess pointed at me again and uttered something in a lilting, unintelligible language.

I felt the magic gather about me, stirring the sky. A web of music, a mist of stars . . .

It began.

Prince Char

We risked everything, my companions and I, in our headlong flight to save Rose. Rather than returning by our safe rat-routes through sewers, pipes, and walls, we ran through the streets, out in the open, keeping watch in case the Lancastyr coach passed us on the way back home.

My gallant band had been promised a dangerous action, and so it turned out to be. Need I remind you that most humans are hostile toward rats?

We evoked shrill screams and hasty flight from some, brutal attacks from others. Yet here was a chance for heroism, and my people rose to the occasion. An innkeeper almost crushed Corncob with a heavy keg. Truffle was able to save him with a clever rush-and-feint maneuver that drew the innkeeper's notice away and allowed Corncob to escape.

After several more close shaves, we arrived unharmed at Lancastyr Manor. In the orange-and-purple glow of the sunset, we saw no carriage awaiting at the front of the grand house. My heart felt as though it might split asunder. We were too late. Somehow, we had missed them.

Nevertheless, I swerved and headed for the stables, hoping that perhaps the ladies had tarried in their preparations and the coach had not yet been sent for. If it were still there, we might prevent them from leaving somchow. I had a wild notion of commanding my followers to spook the horses by leaping up and swinging from their tails. It might even have worked.

In the event, we never had a chance to attempt it.

When we rounded the curve of the drive, we were greeted most unexpectedly by the sight of Lady Rose standing on the neat white gravel. She was not wearing the gold gown the mice had tailored for her; instead, she was arrayed in a luminous greeny-blue creation apparently woven from moonbeams and clouds. It hugged her tiny waist and shifted around her long limbs, the way spray floats across a waterfall.

At the same time, the dress gave off a cool, clear scent. Her hair was spangled with diamonds of blinding brilliance. And my gift of the magnificent deep green emeralds blazed around her arched neck.

But all this finery was outshone by the light of her face.

I could not tear my gaze from her.

Then an unnatural female voice captured my attention. "Now, Rose de Lancastyr, you need a coach to take you to the ball, do you not?"

I turned my head to look. The timbre of the voice was a child's, but it had come from an uncanny woman who gave off a pulsing blue light.

As I watched, this creature rolled a large green melon along the drive. (Not a pumpkin, mind you. It was a melon.) Then she pointed at it and uttered some words I could not understand.

In eerie silence, the melon puffed and swirled. It changed in color and sprouted wheels. Before I could register what was taking place, the thing had become an enormous coach, golden and ornate. At my side as always, Swiss gave a shout of disbelief. Corncob and Beef One, Beef Two, and Beef Three scattered quickly, disappearing before I could find my voice to command them. Only the dauntless Truffle remained behind with Swiss and me.

The strange blue woman—evidently a sorceress—laughed. Then she patted the melon-coach with a fluttering hand. "Such a wonderful conveyance to take you to the ball, my dear—is it not?" she warbled to Rose. "You will need horses to pull it, of course."

Rose did not appear to share the blue lady's amusement. She was staring at the vehicle in stark amazement. It bore the Lancastyr coat of arms.

While Swiss, Truffle, and I stood as still as could be, the terrifying bright gaze of the sorceress roved the yard until it lit upon a group of field mice, cowering behind a hay bale. She pointed at them and spoke a few unrecognizable words.

Without a sound to herald the transformation, the mice began to grow: Their legs and necks stretched, and their tiny nervous mouse-expressions faded. Their useful whip-like tails became swatches of long hair, good only for swishing at flies. In a winking, they lost all semblance of their former selves.

They were horses.

Beside me, Swiss stifled a sound. Truffle gripped him with her tail, in warning or support.

Then the changeable eyes of the sorceress began to move again, searching her surroundings as if she knew what she might find next.

Us.

"Flee!" I cried to my subjects. "Make haste and hide!"

We turned to run toward the kitchen garden, but it was too late. The sorceress had spotted us.

"A coachman and two footmen!" she said, giggling. "That's what you need, Rose de Lancastyr. Ah, how very entertaining you mortals are."

I did not see the pointing finger of the blue lady, but I heard the terrible words. And then it happened.

My body left the ground. I floated up in the air toward Rose. And I began to change.

"Blackie! Not Blackie!" Rose shrieked.

My sleek fur; my streamlined, compact, surefooted shape; my keen vision, my powerful snout, my brilliantly accurate whiskers; my ears so sharp, my teeth so strong—lost, all lost, dropping away from me in a rush of bereavement and bewilderment.

I shot up and out, stretched and pulled and pushed until I stood tall, even taller than the two women before me.

Nearby, Swiss had undergone the same transformation. His rat-body was gone, replaced with that of a human.

We were dressed in lavishly embroidered silk tunics, the finest cashmere hose, and jeweled shoes. There was a belt of large precious sapphires slung about my hips, and both Swiss and I wore rings of gold and silver. The sorceress's idea of proper attire for Rose's footmen was magnificent beyond anything I'd ever beheld.

Swiss blinked at me with light, anguished human eyes. He had a pointed chin and a face made to grin, with a broad nose and mouth. Just like the real Swiss. The rat-Swiss.

"Your Highness!" he wailed.

I tried to smell him, to check that he was unharmed, but could not. This thing called a nose hardly worked at all.

I heard a sound of distress and whirled to see Truffle teetering on her new human legs. They were short and sturdy, more ratlike than mine, and her hair and eyebrows were gray with age. This was the cruelest change indeed: the sorceress had magicked a young female rat into an old human coachman.

"Your Highness, what is happening?" Truffle patted herself gingerly. Shock spread across her face as her new human fingers encountered a superior coachman's cloak. Then she appeared to realize there was something on her head. It was a tricorne hat. She took it off, held it at arm's length, and gazed at it in dumb disbelief.

Anger sparked in my heart. My subjects were being used as pawns in some heartless game of magic, and I hadn't the power to stop it.

Not yet.

But it was my responsibility to take care of Swiss and Truffle.

"Fear nothing, my brave companions," I assured them in the human tongue. "I shall not leave you. I will get you out of this."

"Prince Char," the blue lady called, coming close.

I stiffened my new spine and sinews, instructing myself not to shy away from her.

"What have you done?" I demanded. "Who are you and why have . . ."

She leaned forward and lay her forehead against mine. "Prince Char, noblest of your kind, tonight you will guard Rose de Lancastyr. Say nothing and do nothing to dissuade her from attending this event, for it is there that she will meet, and make, her fate."

But . . . Prince Geoffrey!

I made as if to protest, to pour out my fears in human speech so that Rose could be warned, but to no avail. The sorceress had cast a spell upon me with her words, and my mouth remained shut. So I tried to force my human legs to take me to Rose, in order to carry her into the house and keep her there if necessary, but I could not move.

"Rose de Lancastyr will attend the ball," the blue lady declared, as if she knew my thoughts. "You shall not interfere. I, Ashiira, order it to be."

There was magic in her speech.

Then she put her arms across my shoulders and chanted some more foreign words. Within her embrace, the panic and fury slowly seeped out of me and trickled away.

"You have the form of a man," she whispered. "It is now time to fully become one."

And I did.

I reached toward the twilit sky with arms so long, I thought I might touch it. I took a deep breath and inhaled this new world, then exhaled the old one.

Ahhh.

A powerful tide of cool elation surged through me. In this new shape, I could do much. And I *would* do it. I would save my people from Geoffrey. I would rid them of Wilhemina. I would . . .

"Do as I bid," said Ashiira. "Protect Rose de Lancastyr."

"You need not cast a spell to make me do that," I

replied. "It's what I've always intended. If you desire her safety, then why would you allow—"

She hushed me with a finger to my lips. "Trust me," she said. "I am the spirit of the ring you gave to Rose. The Lancastyrs are your humans. They are my humans, too."

So she was not a sorceress after all—she was the fabled goddess of the Lancastyrs! Why had this not occurred to me? This meant Lady Rose had used the ring, and I was the one responsible for tonight's madness. I'd intended Rose to employ the ring as a fallback if other means failed. Yet I had not meant her to do so alone, without guidance, without consulting the red book I'd been so careful to give her.

None of this had come to pass as I'd anticipated.

The goddess touched me again, and my frantic thoughts dispersed. "Your transformation is not a curse," she whispered, "but a blessing."

"A blessing? How so?"

"Blackie?" Rose's voice, tentative and afraid, came from behind me.

I turned around.

She gasped when she saw my face.

Alas, I must make an ugly human, I thought. *I have frightened her.*

"My name is not Blackie," I said. "It is Char." Then I looked at her, for the very first time, through the eyes of a man.

It was my turn to gasp. In that instant, I understood everything.

I was in love with Rose.

I always had been.

"A blessing," Ashiira repeated, then laughed. The sound was like music, peals of delight.

CINDERELLA

Char stood before me in his new form: tall, lean, almost willowy. His dark eyes were alight with their usual intelligence and sympathy, and a touch of humor lurked at the corners of his mouth.

He smiled. I could not look away from him.

My pet rat.

No, he had never been a pet—I realized that now—nor had he ever been mine. But whatever he was before, he'd become human tonight.

And what a human! I'd never seen a man so beautiful.

If I had ever thought about it, I might have expected a bespelled animal to behave like an empty puppet, without a mind or soul. However, this was clearly not the case with the young man standing before me.

Char.

"Rose de Lancastyr," he said, reaching a slender hand toward mine. "At last the silence between us is broken."

My heart heard much more than his words.

He brushed a kiss across my fingertips as he bowed low. When he looked up, my breath caught. And as his touch lingered, I felt my courage returning.

How did he do it? Char was always able to refresh my spirit, it seemed. Whichever form he took.

"We are together now," he said. "Wherever you go tonight, I shall be watching. You will come to no harm."

His manner was so intense, his deep voice so full of hidden meaning, I was confused. "Why, whatever could harm me at the ball?" I asked.

He seemed as if he were about to speak, then stopped and looked disturbed. He probably thought I was a fool for speaking so inconsequentially to him—he who had become a man because of my careless wish! Could I not have made my first words to him something memorable, now that we were able to talk to each other as humans?

"What are you thinking, my lady?" His brow narrowed with concern beneath his glossy black hair.

"Char, this situation must seem strange to you—it certainly does to me. However, perhaps you and I can discuss—"

"Well, now, children, that's enough of that!" Ashiira said, laughing. "We haven't much time, you know!"

With a few flicks of her wrist, she had Char and Frump-Bum on the back of the coach, the rat-coachman on the driver's perch, the mice-horses harnessed, and me inside, twisting my hands together and biting my lip so as not to scream in frustration.

"Be sure to accomplish everything you need to do before midnight," the goddess ordered, "for at the stroke of twelve, the spell dissolves completely." Then she slapped the hindquarters of the first horse and called out: "To Castle Wendyn!"

Prince Char

As footmen, we stood on small platforms at the back of the carriage, holding on to wooden handles for support while the vehicle jostled along the cobblestone roads of Glassevale. I'd wondered if I might find it difficult to balance in my new shape, but the goddess had given us full human ability.

Truffle clearly remembered which way to go, driving us along at a spanking pace in spite of the fact that darkness had finally fallen. There were running lamps at all four corners of the coach, oil burning in glass to light our way. The people who earlier had chased us and shouted at us when we ran through the streets as rats now cheered the gleaming vehicle and the imposing servants who flanked it.

"This is your fault!" Swiss howled over the noise of the street. "Lady Rose didn't read the part in the book where her ancestor explains about the use of the ring and its power, and now look what's happened!"

"Very well, it's my fault for giving her the ring. Might we move beyond that now?"

"To what?" Swiss prompted. "Are you going to let her go to the castle and fall into the clutches of the mad prince? Why are we escorting her there, of all places? We should order Truffle to drive us far, far away."

"Did you not notice?" I said bitterly. "Ashiira is in charge. Clearly, Rose's ring-wish was to go to the ball. Any attempt to stop her from getting there will be thwarted."

For once, Swiss had nothing to say in reply. I listened to the *clack-clack* of the carriage and the snorting of the horses before coming to a decision.

"Wait here," I told him. Then I turned on my perch and grasped hold of the gilt trim on the side of the coach with my new, versatile fingers and thumbs.

"Stop! You'll fall!" Swiss shouted, but I paid him no heed.

It was amazing. These large human hands allowed

me to inch my way along the running board, then support my weight with one hand while jiggling open a door with the other. When the door swung wide, I inserted my feet through the opening and dropped inside.

"Eeek!" said Rose, shrinking back.

"At last you are properly frightened by a rat, my lady." I smiled at her before turning to close the door. Then I took the velvet-cushioned seat opposite her and leaned forward. "We must talk."

She brightened, smiled back at me, and took my hands in hers. "Oh, Blackie—I mean, Char—look at you! Why, you are so *human*. Does it hurt?"

"No." I tried to think what to tell her first.

She saw my hesitation and misinterpreted it as confusion. "You must be wondering how this came to pass. You also must think I rejected the beautiful gown you gave me! Not so. Wilhemina destroyed it, and left me behind when she took her daughters and my father to the castle."

Outrageous! I suppressed a strong desire to curse.

She squeezed my hands. "I'm sorry the goddess, er, changed you and your friends like that. Please believe me, I did not ask it of her."

The tenderness in her voice gave me an odd feeling

in my chest. "Thank you, Lady Rose. The change was disturbing, unsettling, yet I'm fast becoming used to it." In fact, I was beginning to realize I may have misjudged humans my entire life, which is a hard admission for a rat to make.

"Truly? You're very brave. I was so worried about you," she said with an admiring glance. "And Frump-Bum, too, of course."

"His name is Swiss," I replied absently, my head full of the need to get past Ashiira's spell and warn Rose about Prince Geoffrey. "And the coachman is Truffle. She is—or was—a female. See here, though, we have more weighty matters to discuss." I leaned back and let go of her hands.

Her face fell.

"That is to say," I amended, "I am deeply honored to make your acquaintance in this magical manner, but I must tell you most pressingly—" My tongue ceased to move. I had run up against Ashiira's boundary of bewitchment. "My lady—" I struggled to form my thoughts in a way that could outwit the spell.

"Please call me Rose. After all, we're old friends, you and I."

The interior of the carriage was not large, and her nearness was having a disconcerting effect on my thinking. To be precise, it was most difficult to think at all. So rather than showing appreciation and elaborating upon the theme she'd raised, I said the first thing that sprang to my lips.

"My lady, I appear to the world to be your servant. I believe it is not the done thing for a footman to call his lady by her name."

She sat up. "Very well," she said in a lofty voice. "If you do not wish to be upon familiar terms with me . . . Sir."

This would never do. "On the contrary, Rose. I shall use your name in private, with great joy."

At that she laughed, grew a bit pink, and then gave me a confused look. "You called me your lady. How do you know about proper forms of address, and . . . and everything? You have been a, well, a rat."

"We rats know your world. We watch. We listen."

"So every one of you understands human speech?"

"Some of us can even read."

"Of course you read. I ought to have realized! You gave me my ancestor's book and showed me the relevant passage. My goodness, Char. How could I have been so blind to the fact that you and your people are, well . . . people? I fear I've been quite foolish."

"No, no, my lady, do not say such things." I reached out to touch her hair. It was fine as spun sugar. I quickly dropped my hand. "You deserve great praise. You are resourceful and persevering—like a rat."

She blushed and appeared pleased with my compliments.

I would have given her more of them, but this was not the moment. We were hurtling toward potential disaster. I needed information, and I needed it now. I reasoned that although the goddess had forbidden me to prevent Rose from attending the ball, I would nonetheless be allowed to question her. "My lady, do you truly desire to marry Prince Geoffrey?" There. The spell had not stopped me from asking. I'd been right.

The pleasure left Rose's face and she folded her arms across her chest, while I felt the collar around my human neck getting uncomfortably tight.

Then she replied, "Before today, I might have considered marriage with Prince Geoffrey if it turned out that we were suited, because it would solve my family's worries. But I could not marry him now in any case."

My heart leapt. "Why not?"

Her eyes widened. "Need you ask? Just look at

what the goddess Ashiira has done!" She glanced down at her shimmering self. "I would be ashamed to marry someone who fell in love not with me, but with an enchantment. To ensnare a man's heart without his free will—why, it's the sort of thing my stepmother would do. In fact, it's exactly what she did to my dear, confused papa."

"I assure you, Prince Geoffrey does not require or deserve your sympathy. Rather, *urgh*—"

Canines and cattails! Ashiira had stopped my mouth again.

Rose misinterpreted my sudden silence. "Are you in pain? Perhaps you require time to get used to your new, er, human mouth."

Time was just what we didn't have. "Rose, I wish to be your champion. How might I best serve you tonight?"

"Thank you! I am in the most desperate trouble, Char," she said. "You are aware of how bad things have been since Wilhemina came to Lancastyr Manor."

"Yes, indeed," I said with feeling.

"At the ball, I hope to find someone to help save my father—maybe even the prince himself will come to my aid."

Stay away from him! I wanted to shout.

"And there is more," she continued. "While you were a rat—listening and watching, as you say—did you ever overhear the rumors that my stepmother might have had a hand in her first husband's death?"

"What?" I gasped. "No." I wondered how on earth we'd missed this.

She quickly explained, and suddenly a number of things made sense that had seemed mysterious before. "So that is why you hang about the kitchens!"

"Yes." She nodded. "Did you, like everyone else, think me a coward and a cloth-head?"

I coughed and avoided the question. "Rose, I honor you. You are most courageous and intelligent and— Wait, let us think."

She tilted her head to the side, causing her silky hair to dangle in fetching loops.

I forced myself not to gaze at her openmouthed like a fool. Instead I said, "I think you cannot expect help from Prince Geoffrey if he falls in love with you, and then you reject his hand in marriage. He will likely be angry." *And I shall break his neck if he tries to take a sword to yours.*

"Hmm." She appeared to consider this. "I'm afraid you're right. Still, if my father's old friends Sir Tompkin and Lord Bluehart are there, we may approach them instead of the prince."

I replied, "I don't think so, my lady. We rats noticed that those 'friends' never even took the trouble to visit you after your father remarried. Why would they help us now? Let us instead take decisive, permanent action. You lure Lady Wilhemina out to the darkest part of the garden, where Swiss and Truffle and I will be waiting. We'll dispatch her and leave her in the bushes. No one will suspect us. And even if they did catch us, what could they do once we turn back into rats at midnight?"

"Char!" she shrieked. "You cannot mean to kill her?"

I stared. "Of course."

"But you must not."

She took hold of my shoulders and brought her delicately curved face right up to mine. This had a dizzying effect.

"Char, I understand you want to help me, and that you want to be rid of Wilhemina to protect your fellow rats. As for the latter, Wilhemina does not realize that rats have souls and personalities of their own. She doesn't think of killing rats as murder."

I clamped down on my emotions. I already was cognizant of these unhappy facts and replied with bitterness, "But my people are in fear for their lives, Rose."

"You speak truly, and Wilhemina must be stopped. But some other way. Think of Jessamyn, and even the dreadful Eustacia. They would be orphaned," she said.

I hardened my heart. "Better to have no mother than a mother like that one."

"Do you think Jessamyn and Eustacia would agree?"

I said nothing. She hadn't convinced me. The more I considered it, the more I was sure that Ashiira had given me human form in order to save the house of Lancastyr as well as my fellow rats.

How could Rose not see?

I heard Ashiira's voice in my memory: *Become a man.* I thought I'd understood what she had meant, but perhaps there was more to it.

"As you wish," I said at last. "I will not take Wilhemina's life tonight, nor will Swiss or Truffle." The words were carefully chosen, for I already had a notion of who might be maneuvered into carrying out justice this evening if I played the game with precision. "Instead, I will help you seek aid from your father's friends to rid ourselves of Wilhemina. How do you propose to get me inside the castle?"

She narrowed her eyes, assessing me. "Your attire is so fine, you can certainly pass as a gentleman. Remain inside the carriage here with me. When we arrive, I shall introduce you as my very distant cousin, from a far kingdom, whose ways are somewhat strange."

"Will being your distant relation allow me to follow you wherever you go?"

"It depends." She arched a brow. "Perhaps we should make you a member of the nobility for tonight. What honorary title shall we give you?"

"I already have a title," I answered. "A real one."

"You do?"

Her surprise was somewhat insulting. "I am Prince Char, ruler of the Northern Rat Realm."

Her huge eyes, a far clearer green than the emeralds about her neck, grew even larger. "You are a prince?"

"*The* prince. There is never a king of the rats. Or, you might say, the prince is the king. And that would be me."

I waited for her reaction to this news. I'd hoped at

least for an *Oh, Char, how marvelous!* or perhaps, *Well done, you!*

But after a few moments elapsed and it seemed she would make no comment, I concealed my disappointment and said, "Right, then. Is there any human kingdom called the Northern Realm of which you are aware?"

"No," she said in a faint voice.

"Then we will be safe. I shall mingle with the humans and use a slight variation of my real title, Prince of the Northern Realm. Allow me to inform Swiss, my royal councillor, of our plans."

I made as if to return the way I'd come, but she grabbed my coat to hold me back. "Forgive me," she said, "but you cannot mean to climb out there again?"

"Why not?" I shrugged. "It was quite enjoyable the first time."

"I shall ask the driver to stop," she said.

"If you insist."

She did so, and I took a moment to let Swiss, Truffle, and even the mice-horses know what we were up to. I instructed Swiss to follow me and Rose into the castle, in the guise of my personal guard. As a precaution, I had Swiss switch his tunic with Truffle, to make us look less like a matched set of footmen, and I untied the ribbon holding back my queue, letting the longish dark locks fall about my shoulders. Then I reentered the carriage with my lady, and we approached the castle at a more sedate pace.

There was a strange quiet between us. I was sorry for it. "Have I offended you in some way, Rose?"

"Oh, no, Your Highness."

"I thought we'd agreed to call each other by our first names when alone."

"Prince Char, why did you give me the magic ring?"

"I wanted to comfort you and give you courage."

"Yes, Char, but why?"

Had she not figured it out yet? Even though she had no real sense of smell or the aid of sensitive whiskers, I should think the truth would have been more than obvious to her by now.

"Because you are as kind and noble as the best of rats," I began.

"Oh!" she cried. Her hand went to her breast.

I hesitated. Was that a good sort of *Oh*, or a bad sort of *Oh*? Should I go on, or should I leave my deepest feelings unsaid?

The coach came slowly to a stop. I moved aside the blue silk curtain from the window and saw looming stone towers, blazing torches, and many well-dressed people being helped from their conveyances.

I looked over at her. I could not read her expression. "I did not know it at the time, but there was another reason I gave you the ring. I am in love with you, Rose. My heart is yours."

Her apple-pink lips parted and she drew in a breath.

I added: "And may I just say, I quite admire those pretty glass slippers."

CINDERELLA

He loves me.

The handsome, dashing, noble prince I had always dreamt of was sitting right across from me in this coach.

He'd befriended me when I was a menial in my own father's house, and he'd given me everything in his capacity to give. Kindness, loyalty, hope, food. When he told me why he admired me, he had mentioned not my beauty, but my character.

He loves me.

And witness his bravery! Thrust into a man's body and a human world, he seemed confident of his ability to master whatever came his way. His concern was not for himself, but for me and the lives of his people.

He was everything a girl could ask for.

He also happened to be a rat.

Earlier, when Char had boldly reached out and touched my hair with tender reverence, I'd made no protest, though I doubtless should have.

I shivered with secret delight.

He is in love with me.

But before I could respond to his declaration, the doors of the coach were flung open, the steps were unfolded, and Swiss handed me down to the red carpet leading up the grand staircase of Castle Wendyn.

As I emerged from the coach, there was a collective intake of breath among the ballgoers. After a moment of awed silence, there followed a cascade of whispered comment, swelling with each step I took up the stairs. By the time Char and I reached the landing where the majordomo awaited to announce the guests, the comments were loud enough for me to hear.

"My dear, who is she?"

"She is glorious! Magnificent!"

"Beautiful, so beautiful. Have you ever seen the like?"

You may have thought I would have felt embarrassed at the fulsome praise; yet it was the goddess's magic they were speaking of, not the real Rose de Lancastyr. I only wished I could take some pleasure in this evidence that the enchantment was working. Instead, it unsettled me.

My stepmother was somewhere in this throng, hating me, as was Eustacia. I felt myself begin to panic. What if she questioned the claim that Char and I were distant kin? Then at the small of my back came Char's firm, warm touch, as if he could sense my fears.

He murmured one word in my ear: "Courage."

My true friend. I wanted to hold him in my arms, and be held by him against his noble heart.

"I shall always be at your side, my lady," he whispered.

Then the enormous clock set into the tallest tower of the castle began to toll the hour of eight, and I remembered Ashiira's words: *At the stroke of twelve, the spell dissolves completely.* A bolt of dread shot through my breast.

Char would *not* always be at my side! In a mere four hours, he would become a rat again and return to his own realm.

"Whom shall I announce?" the majordomo asked.

Char replied, staring straight ahead, "His Royal Highness, Prince Char of the Northern Realm, and the great-grandchild of his mother's father's sister's cousin's uncle by marriage, Rose de Lancastyr." His eyelashes were an extravagant fringe of black, his mouth a clean line with a happy quirk. He appeared to be quite enjoying himself.

The majordomo wavered for a moment. "The name is . . . Char? Did I hear aright, Your Highness?"

"Short for *Charming*," I corrected, relieved that I was still able to speak in spite of my nerves. "Prince Charming."

Char's glance caught mine, and for a moment I thought he might laugh at the name I'd just given him. But he only smiled as the fellow boomed our titles across the splendid room. There was a musician's gallery of carved, polished fruitwood at one end, from which the strains of a lovely violin piece were issuing. Massive pink marble columns supported a high ceiling painted aqua with gold stars. And suspended from the ceiling like a brilliant constellation was the largest chandelier I had ever seen, sparkling with what looked like a thousand lit candles, directly above the king's throne.

Char glanced up at the chandelier. Then he threw

a look over his shoulder at Swiss, who raised a grim brow.

"What is it, Char?" I whispered.

"A mere nothing," he said.

The landing where we stood was a perfect place from which to view the glittering throng. I caught sight of Wilhemina with her red tiara, shooing my stepsisters and my father into a distant corner. As I watched, she threw me a venomous look and began speaking rapidly behind her fan to her crony, Lady Harriet.

My heart beat faster.

Then Char and I, with Swiss at our backs, made a slow, gracious descent of the staircase into the ballroom. All talking stopped, all eyes turned our way, and the guests moved aside to leave a wide path for us, leading straight up to the royal throne. There sat Good King Tumtry, in ermine robes and jeweled crown. Next to him stood a handsome young man I recognized as the prince. He wore a scarlet silk doublet, a red velvet cape, and a slender circlet of twisted gold upon his head. Slung across his chest was a belt from which hung a gleaming sword. His pose was somewhat drooped, as if from discouragement. But when he caught sight of me, he straightened and moved forward to place a hand upon his father's shoulder.

It seemed a sweet gesture, showing a bond between father and son.

"Careful, my lady," whispered Char. "We both need our wits about us tonight."

I felt unsteady. However, there seemed to be magic in my glass slippers. They gave spring to my steps, and Char supported me imperceptibly with his arm.

We drew nearer. Prince Geoffrey's attractive face lit up in a flashing smile.

So many large white teeth.

"By the Rood!" he cried. "The fairest of them all! My lady—what did the majordomo say? Rose de Lancastyr, your beauty blinds my eyes, enthralls my heart, renders me speechless!"

I heard a small sound from Char that could only have been a snort. "That sounded like a vast deal of speech to me," he whispered.

Then Prince Geoffrey bounded forward and took my hand, pulling me toward his father. There was a moment's tiny struggle as Char refused to give up his hold on my arm, and Geoffrey darted a frown at him.

Char let go with distinct reluctance.

"Father, Father," Prince Geoffrey babbled. "How is it I have never before seen this goddess of love and beauty? What need for a ball, or a search, when perfection has been so close at hand all along?"

Apparently, Geoffrey had not noticed me at my debut when I was fifteen, though he'd made quite an impression on me.

"Lady Rose," King Tumtry said with a smile of welcome, though he remained seated upon his throne. "you are indeed a vision of loveliness."

I curtsied low, thanking him and saying something about not being worthy of such a tribute.

Prince Geoffrey bowed with a twirly wave of one hand. "Lady Rose, you are far too modest. You're as fetching as your floral namesake. Why, you even smell like a rose!"

I quickly controlled my expression. I wished Char had not been standing quite so close to me with *such* a look upon his face! If I burst into inappropriate laughter, what cause would that serve?

Prince Geoffrey did not seem to notice, thank heavens.

"So, my dear," the king said to me, "this is your royal relation, Prince Charming?" He gave a regal nod to Char, then addressed him directly. "I'm not familiar with the Northern Realm, Your Highness, yet you are most welcome here. I look forward to learning more about you and your people this evening."

Char made a stylish bow—not too low, simply a respectful inclination in the king's direction, as was appropriate from one monarch to another. I couldn't help but notice the silky tumble of fine dark hair over his forehead as he moved.

"Your Majesty," he said. "I'm honored. You may not know the Northern Realm, but your royal wisdom and the keenness of your councillors, Lord Hamp and Lord Brimfield, is legendary even in my far-distant land. Perhaps later I may obtain your advice on a problem that has been vexing me, if you would be so kind."

I was impressed again. How on earth had Char learned the names of the royal councillors?

King Tumtry perked up a bit and looked at Char with genuine interest. "This pleases me greatly!" he said. "My privy council and I would be glad to guide you howsoever we may. In fact, Brimfield and Hamp are right here." He beckoned two distinguished-looking older lords forward.

"Prince Charming has expressed a desire for our

counsel," the king informed his advisers. "How rare these days to find a young man with great responsibility who seeks, rather than rejects, the advice of his elders." He gave a sidelong glance toward his son, then looked again at Char. "Are you, like my son, Prince Geoffrey, heir apparent to the throne of your kingdom?"

"No, Your Majesty." Char folded his hands behind his back with a wisp of a smile. "In my realm, the prince is sovereign."

"Now that is interesting," Prince Geoffrey chimed in.

King Tumtry exchanged looks with Lord Brimfield and Lord Hamp.

Then Lord Hamp asked Char, "How long ago did you inherit, Your Highness?"

"In my land the throne is not inherited, but earned by trial. We have an old saying in the Northern Realm: 'Monarch is best who passes the test.' I earned the princedom several years ago. Though perhaps for modesty's sake, I should not have mentioned it."

King Tumtry's sad gaze lightened. He admired Char already; I could tell.

So, unfortunately, could Prince Geoffrey.

Geoffrey frowned, then darted a few looks between Char and me, as though trying to figure out if Char had stolen my heart as well as the king's. I strove to keep my expression neutral.

"I would be fascinated to hear more about a country that allows only the worthy to rule," King Tumtry said to Char.

"Yes, a most engaging and perhaps useful topic," Lord Brimfield agreed.

"Nay, it is boring!" Prince Geoffrey exclaimed. "Why do we discuss dull subjects like rulership in front of a glorious lady, when we're here to enjoy ourselves?"

"Indeed, this discussion is wasted upon some of us," the king said with a pointed frown. Though I found this rather shocking, it seemed to go over Prince Geoffrey's head.

"Exactly, Father," he agreed. "This is a ball, and though everyone else has been dancing and feasting, I have not. Now that you've come, beautiful lady, there shall be jollity!"

King Tumtry looked exasperated and somewhat worried. My gaze met Char's, and he seemed to be trying to convey something to me without words. Was it another warning? I took a deep breath. Then I let Prince Geoffrey take my hand and lead me out to the floor. Though I'd only just arrived at the ball, here I was, dancing with the prince. My emotions should have been soaring as high as the shining chandelier.

"Musicians!" he called up to the gallery. "A sprightly tune for the queen of my heart!" The music began, and Prince Geoffrey swung me into a lively dance.

His grip on my shoulder was uncomfortably tight.

Prince Char

"**A** sprightly tune for the queen of my heart!"

I struggled against a strong impulse to wrap my now-nonexistent tail around Prince Geoffrey's neck.

And I was not the only one angered by his attitude.

King Tumtry's brows were drawn tightly together, his hands clenched.

I looked over toward my faithful Swiss, who remained still as a soldier a few steps away. I said, "Guard, please follow my cousin and keep her safe. Use whatever means necessary. Do not leave her side."

Swiss gave me a look of understanding, saluted, and complied.

When Prince Geoffrey's dance with Rose had finished, the orchestra commenced to play another. Lord Hamp finally said, "Prince Charming, you show a most brotherly concern for Lady Lancastyr."

Brotherly? How very amusing. "Lord Hamp and Lord Brimfield, I have left my young relative alone for too long since her mother died. I was not aware that her father is wandering in his wits and incapable of protecting her from harm. So now I feel I should ask you the questions about Prince Geoffrey that a father might ask."

"Er, ask away," Lord Hamp said.

"My lords, though you are known as wise and just leaders, I have heard nothing at all about Prince Geoffrey except that he is handsome . . . and some uneasy whisperings about his character. Should not the people know more of their crown prince? Why do I get a strong impression of truths concealed?"

"Why, whatever can you mean? We are concealing nothing, Your Highness!" blustered Lord Brimfield.

"Are you not?" I glanced at King Tumtry, who seemed more than ever ill at ease. How far dare I push? "Then the gossip I overheard is untrue?"

"There is no gossip! I have made sure of—" Lord

Brimfield began, but Lord Hamp held out a hand to him in a silencing move.

"Gossip usually is untrue, Prince Charming," Hamp smoothly said. "I'm surprised a prince like you would stoop to listen."

I gave a light laugh. "Bravo, Lord Hamp, well done. Your king is most fortunate in his councillors. I can see I will need to be blunt. The problem I mentioned earlier, which has been vexing me and upon which I need your advice, is a simple one: Pray tell, is my cousin safe with Prince Geoffrey?"

Knowing what I knew, I wondered how he could possibly answer.

Apparently, Lord Hamp was wondering the same thing, for he remained silent just a few ticks too long.

Then King Tumtry surprised us by growling, "Oh, have done with this pretense. Prince Charming is intelligent indeed, and he has obviously figured out the truth we've been able to hide from the entire kingdom." He then turned to me and said, "Prince Charming, I do not understand my son; he has become selfish, violent, and frightening. I ask myself where my dear queen and I went astray in the raising of him. I wish I had not allowed this ball to go forward, for its premise is wicked. But I am advanced in years, feeble and holding on to life and rulership as long as I can until we find a solution. We meant to find a wise and, er, calm young lady to marry Geoffrey. One who could rule as queen if Geoffrey's situation does not improve . . . and who might bear him a worthy son or daughter to inherit the throne."

"You wish to sacrifice my cousin's safety and happiness for the sake of the kingdom," I ruthlessly corrected him.

Lord Hamp and Lord Brimfield both began to speak at once, then glared each other down.

"I feel for your dilemma, gentlemen," I declared after a breath of tense silence, "yet I cannot in good conscience allow my cousin to be matched with a dangerous man. I would like to resolve this peaceably. May I leave the problem in your hands?"

"I'm deeply sorry, Prince Charming," Lord Brimfield said. "But it looks like Prince Geoffrey has fallen head over heels in love with Lady Rose. Once he makes up his mind, no one is ever able to persuade him to change it, no matter how hard we try."

"And if we tried, we would bring on one of his, er, *turns*," Lord Hamp warned, unable to repress a grimace.

An image of Quintilius Porter's head, rolling on the floor, flashed into my mind.

"Let us humor my son tonight," King Tumtry said with great weariness. "We'll allow him to think he can become engaged to Lady Rose. Then tomorrow, when your cousin is gone—perhaps even on her way to the Northern Realm with you, Prince Charming—I shall inform him I do not approve of the match."

I considered this notion. It had the elegance of simplicity, and the advantage of not exposing Rose and the party guests to a potentially lethal temper tantrum from Prince Geoffrey. Though unfortunately, I had no far realm to which I could whisk Rose away. So it was more crucial than ever that we find her father's old friends tonight, if possible, so they could pick up where I would have to leave off.

"I agree," I said. "In the meantime, my guard will protect Lady Rose."

"Very well," said the king. "And of course, if any trouble should emerge, my own guard is here to intervene."

I bowed to King Tumtry. "Thank you, Your Majesty."

Lord Brimfield said, with feeling, "Prince Charming, we owe you thanks for understanding our situation. It is most compassionate and humane of you."

I wondered if he would be so full of admiration for my humanity (ha!) had he known what I was planning. I gave a glance to the clock on the musicians' gallery and noted with unease that it was almost the hour of nine. We had but three more hours to set everything right.

"You are indeed admirable, Prince Charming," Lord Hamp added.

Before they could heap any more unearned compliments upon me, a girl I had never seen before interrupted us. I felt relief, until I realized what she was after.

"Beg pardon, Your Majesty, Your Highness, my lords." This girl wore a ruffled candy floss–pink gown with a plunging neckline. She curtsied prettily (though nowhere near as well as Lady Rose could). "My friends and I were wondering if Prince Charming might wish to take the floor with any of us."

I recoiled when I saw a group of giggling young ladies a few feet behind her. "Thank you, but I had really rather not." I hoped my distaste wasn't obvious.

Lord Brimfield said in a low voice, "You will not

wish to insult the local families, Your Highness. I advise you to go."

"I regret," I said in a last-ditch effort, "that I have never learned your local dances!"

"I shall be pleased to teach you," said the pink-gowned creature.

"Go, Prince Charming," King Tumtry said with a glint of a genuine smile. "You are young. Enjoy the ball."

Oh, so be it.

I put one hand at the girl's waist and led her into the dance. Aha, it was easy! The only requirements were to move to the music and imitate what the other dancers were doing. *One, two, three ... one, two, three ...* Then I realized I could steer my partner in the direction of my beloved Rose. We wove in and out of the other couples as I kept her in sight. I noted that Swiss was lurking within a few paces of her at all times.

Then suddenly, there was the dreaded Wilhemina. She and her companions, all dripping with showy jewelry and with their hair piled high on their heads, were grouped around a dessert table, mouths moving rapidly. I guessed they were chewing up my love's reputation as fast as they were gobbling up sweets. I sorely missed my rat-hearing.

And my rat teeth.

But mindful of my promise to Rose, and not wishing to face possibly awkward questions from Wilhemina, I hastened to put as much distance between myself and the loathsome woman as possible, with a few improvised twists and turns.

"What are you doing?" the girl in my arms asked with scarce-concealed annoyance.

"Too many things," I replied.

I searched once more for Rose and saw her still in Geoffrey's arms, her eyes shifting nervously about as if looking for something. When our glances met over the heads of the dancers, she relaxed. Then her gaze moved to the girl I was with.

Instantaneously, Rose seemed to give off sparks.

It could not be jealousy I saw in her face, could it?

I swung my pink-gowned partner about in an arc, which caused her to throw her head back and laugh; then I looked over at my lady again. There was no mistaking it: She was annoyed.

She hadn't said anything earlier in the coach when I'd told her I loved her, so I considered this an encouraging development.

The music abruptly stopped. "Thank you. Er, goodbye," I said to my dance partner. Ignoring her miffed expression, I tried to push my way through the crowd to reach Rose before the next set began. However, my steps were blocked by simpering young females, angling for my escort. I resisted the urge to drop to the floor on all fours and dart between their legs to reach my goal more quickly.

Thus I had made it only as far as Swiss's side before the orchestra struck up a lively tarantella, and Geoffrey led Rose away again.

"No problems yet," Swiss said as I drew close.

But just when I felt a flash of relief, Geoffrey led Rose off the floor and outside the open archway to the lantern-hung courtyard, where there was more dancing.

"Let's go, Swiss." I grabbed his arm, and we followed. Prince Geoffrey began looping Rose around a spurting fountain, at the center of which stood a ridiculous statue of Geoffrey himself, draped with a purple velvet cape.

Oh. *That* statue. It was unsettling to see Geoffrey prancing about in its shadow, with no apparent memory of Quintilius Porter to impair his enjoyment.

"Swiss," I said, "I don't feel comfortable letting Rose spend so much time in that man's arms. But at least I have the king's promise she won't be pressured into marrying him when you and I turn back into rats again. Ah—what's this?"

It was a servant, bearing a large tray of delicacies. He dropped to one knee before me and offered it up. My stomach rumbled; becoming human was a hungry business.

"Your Royal Highness, if it pleases you to partake?" the servant said.

Oh, it pleased me well. For once in my life, a human was offering me food that wasn't laced with a toxic substance. I lifted a piping-hot meat pasty with the intention of popping it into my mouth, then stopped short. What of Swiss? As my supposed underling, he would not be expected to eat these dainties, and therefore would go empty tonight. With a passing thought as well for my poor rat-warrior Truffle, forced to stay outside as a coachman, I handed the pasty to my royal councillor.

"My personal guard tastes all my food before I consume it," I explained to the shocked-looking servant. "Does your king not have a royal taster?"

Swiss did his tasting job with efficient dispatch. First the pasty, then a trio of quail's eggs coddled in rum, then a custard embellished with peaches and crème Chantilly went down the hatch. He and I would have eaten the entire plateful of nibbles, had I not recalled that this was not the human custom, and stopped myself in time.

Swiss and I exchanged satisfied looks. Oh, we could definitely get used to this. Such a shame we only had a few hours left.

Only a few more hours before becoming a rat again, nevermore to talk to Lady Rose de Lancastyr. Never to stroke her hair, or feel her hand in mine.

"Your Highness?"

I turned toward the voice. There before me stood a slight elderly gentleman in sober, dark clothing and a white wig. He made a very fancy bow when I acknowledged him.

"I am Sir Tompkin Mayfield, Your Highness, friend of Lady Rose's father, Barnaby de Lancastyr," he said.

I looked Sir Tompkin up and down. I recognized his merry countenance (though currently it was grave as a coffin) from his many visits to Lancastyr Manor in the old days. Disapproval washed over me. This man had not turned out to be much of a friend, had he?

"Sir Tompkin," I said as politely as I could. "Lady Rose wishes to meet with you." I drew him away from the dancing, toward the lawn. Swiss came, too, though his eyes kept tracking my lady.

Sir Tompkin said, "Wonderful, Your Highness, for I most devoutly wish to see Rose! And so does my companion Lord Bluehart, though I seem to have lost him. I excused myself for a moment, and when I came back I couldn't find him in this crowd."

When I answered him, my manner was austere. "This eagerness to communicate seems quite a change for you and Lord Bluehart, for Lady Rose tells me you've not visited her or Lord Lancastyr even once since he married Lady Wilhemina."

To my dismay, Sir Tompkin became teary-eyed and drew a large handkerchief from his coat, then blew into it loudly. "Oh dear me, this is most unnerving. *Most* distressing! Bluehart and I have been quite exercised over it. We tried to visit, Your Highness, I assure you we did! There is apparently much amiss at Lancastyr Manor. If we'd known Barnaby had a relation in another land, we would have contacted you as soon as we believed something was wrong!"

Perhaps he and Bluehart weren't the dastards I'd considered them. "Tell me what you mean, Sir Tompkin."

"It's so terrible," he said. "When we saw our friend

Barnaby here this evening, we were optimistic that we might finally speak with him. We approached him—and he did not even seem to recognize us! Then his harpy of a wife spurned our friendly advances and led him away."

He seemed about to say more, but we were interrupted by a yelp of surprise from Swiss. "Prince Char!"

I leapt to Swiss's side and gripped his shoulder. "What's wrong? Is Lady Rose in danger?"

"No, my prince." He rolled his eyes in Sir Tompkin's direction. "Begging your pardon, but may I speak to you in private, Your Highness?"

"Sir Tompkin, will you excuse us for a moment?" Still with my hand clamped on Swiss's shoulder, we moved away. "This had better be good."

"It's not good—it's bad. I just saw your mother."

"What? Lady Apricot, here?"

"Back there, inside the ballroom. She's hiding underneath the table where the punch bowl is. See— over in the corner. And she has her ladies with her."

Oh, good gravy. Just what I needed.

I made a frustrated sound through clenched teeth. "I'll be right back. Don't let Sir Tompkin get away, and don't let Geoffrey hurt Lady Rose, agreed?"

He nodded.

I made my excuses to a bewildered Sir Tompkin and headed toward the punch bowl, where a stiffly starched lackey handed me a full cup of punch.

"Oops!" I deliberately let it drop to the floor.

When I stooped to pick it up (in a most unprincely manner), I hissed into the tablecloth: "Mother, I know you're under there! Meet me in the gardens right away, or I shall see to it you never eat another apricot in your life."

The ensuing sounds of botheration told me she would leave as I demanded.

And not a moment too soon, for a host of servants had joined me on the floor, insisting I should not sully my royal hands; they would clean up the spill. So I left them to it.

I returned to the courtyard to rejoin the others, and noticed Rose was looking rather seasick, still dancing with Prince Geoffrey. It was time to end this farce. I strode up to Geoffrey and tapped his shoulder. "May I cut in?"

His glare was equal parts anger and surprise. I wondered if anyone had ever dared interrupt his pleasures in his entire life. Had I taken a misstep? Would Geoffrey lose his temper too early in the evening, before I could channel it in the right direction?

No. Rose averted the danger with a dazzling display of rat-like wiles. "Ah, my cousin Charming! Have you come to escort me to sit out the next set? I declare I am quite dizzy! The great honor done to me by Prince Geoffrey has overwhelmed my senses and I fear I might faint."

I thought she might be overdoing it just a little. However, the smugness dawning in Geoffrey's smile meant he took such exaggeration as his due.

"Yes, Cousin Rose." I smiled, taking her hand. "Come, rest for a bit in the gardens with me. I hope you'll pardon us, Your Highness?"

Before Geoffrey could react, he was mobbed by a swarm of young lady predators. "Prince Geoffrey, I should love to have the next waltz!" I heard one say. Then came the cry: "Not her, Prince Geoffrey, choose *me*!"

Rose and I took advantage of his momentary distraction to move across the courtyard and disappear into the flower garden beyond.

"Thank you for the rescue," she said as we left the noisy throng behind us. "I was on the brink of collapse. The prince heeded none of my gentle hints to sit out a dance! Do you know, Char, I begin to think there is something quite wrong with him."

How I wished Ashiira would allow me to comment!

We passed through a vine-covered archway and came to a standstill in the middle of a circle of well-tended floral beds. The air was heavy with the perfume of roses, enveloping us in a sense of privacy and promise. Only the light of the moon and the gentle fairy glow of her dress illuminated the scene, as I looked down at her.

"Char?" She moistened her lips and murmured, "I am glad to be here with you."

"Thank you, my dear Rose," I said. "Your words give me hope." Well, there was no hope for me, when it came to her. "I mean, happiness."

She drew nearer. Faint strains of music filtered across the garden from the castle. I longed to pull her into an embrace.

Instead I took her hand and said, "I have good news. Your father's friend, Sir Tompkin, approached me while you were dancing, and he wants to see you."

The mood was broken. "Sir Tompkin? He is here? This is marvelous! Surely Lord Bluehart is with him?" She stepped back and looked up at me.

Then we were both startled by the loud sound of a stomach growling.

It was hers. She clapped two delicate hands across her small midsection.

We looked at each other; then we both began to laugh.

"I'm sorry, Char," she said. "As Pye would say, my stomach is sticking to my ribs. I must find some food soon."

Food. Find the Food! "Lady Rose, you would make an excellent rat."

"You, Prince Char, make an excellent human." She wandered over to a rosebush and fingered a blossom. "Don't you wish tonight would never end?"

Of course I did. "Why?"

"So you could stay human forever."

My heart stopped, then began beating again, much harder.

Stay human. Yes. But how?

"There is no chance of it, Rose. You heard what the goddess decreed: at midnight, I ..." I could not say it.

"It can't be true!" She abandoned the blossoms and flung herself toward me. She grasped both of my hands and gave an impassioned cry: "Char, I did not answer you in the coach. But I will answer now: I love you, too."

I did then what I had wanted to do from the first. I closed the space between us and wrapped my arms about her tightly.

Who knows what might have happened next, had I not heard Swiss's human voice calling me: "Your Highness? Are you there? I have Sir Tompkin with me. He wishes to converse with you and my lady. Your Highness?"

"Yoo-hoo!" It was Sir Tompkin. "Lady Rose?"

Damnation. I had one night as a man with the creature I loved—one night only—which I was condemned to spend in the middle of a pack of humans with no concept of personal space. And Swiss had just become the worst of them all!

Rose sprang away from me, then greeted her family friend as he emerged from behind a privet hedge. Much kissing of cheeks followed, many endearments and heartfelt protestations of continuing friendship.

I watched until I heard a telltale chattering in the nearby hydrangea bushes. Sink me! There was no mistaking the dulcet tones of Lady Apricot. Had she and her ladies' maids just been witnesses to my tender scene with Rose? But it was my fault—I had asked her to meet me in the gardens.

"Drat," I muttered. "Swiss, please bring Lady Rose food and drink. She is famished. Now I must be off, though I shall return soon."

I turned and found my way down a dark path, deeper into the gardens, where no one would notice the great Prince Charming of the Northern Realm carrying on a conversation with three large, glossy rats.

CINDERELLA

So many emotions, so little time to sort them out!

Char left us without a backward glance, heading rather mysteriously down a side pathway. I wondered what could possibly take precedence over participating in this long-awaited conversation with Sir Tompkin. Then I recalled Char's earlier mention of luring my stepmother into the gardens and disposing of her there.

No, Char could not be on such a mission. How could I even begin to suspect it? He'd promised not to kill her, and I believed him. He was an honorable man ... rat ... both.

"Come, Sir Tompkin," I said in the brightest voice I could manage. "Here is a quiet seat where we will not be disturbed." We settled onto a bench under the spilling white blooms of a clematis vine.

"Dear, dear little Rose," he said, as if these were still my childhood days when he and Lord Bluehart used to come smoke horrible cigars with my father long into the night, arguing court politics and laughing uproariously until my mother broke it up. His compassionate gray eyes were so familiar, so soothing.

"Sir Tompkin, how I've missed you! Where is Bluey?" I looked over his shoulder in perplexity, as I had never seen one of them without the other.

He made an uncertain gesture. "Heaven knows. I've been seeking him for a good half hour. But not to worry; he will find us soon, and how ecstatic he will be to see you once more!"

I could not hold back my sad question any longer. "Dear sir, why did you and Lord Bluehart not answer any of my letters?"

"Bless my soul!" he exclaimed. "So you tried to contact us, did you? I am sorry, Rose, but we never received a single line from you. The treacherous Wilhemina must have had a hand in that."

Though this only confirmed my suspicions, I felt a flare of fury. While I struggled to control it, Sir

Tompkin said, "Now tell me, young lady, what in the name of Saint Sophy's Seat has been going on at Lancastyr Manor since your father remarried?"

This question would have taken many hours to answer properly. So I confined myself to summing up the past year of suffering in only a few sentences. As I did so, I watched his pleasant face grow longer and longer. He was so overset, I finished the story without revealing my worst suspicions about my stepmother being a murderess. That much, too, was merely hearsay.

While I hesitated, Sir Tompkin plunged into shocked speech. "A terrible tale, by Gad! My poor child, what you have been through!" He drew out a monogrammed handkerchief and mopped tears from his face. "Now see here, Rose," he said. "Lord Bluehart and I tried again and again to visit Lancastyr Manor—always bringing my little dog, Dandle, with us, for you know how much your father always loved to play with him—but we were turned away each time like pestering peddlers!"

"Oh no! I assure you, it was not my father nor I who turned you away."

"Of course not. We knew who must be responsible, yet we could not fathom what to do. Your stepmother even sent word through the servants that you, child, were still too wrapped up in grief over your mother to see anyone or go anywhere." He frowned. "I realize now that Bluey and I ought to have shown up at your home with outriders and carried you off by main force a long time ago. Saved you from that harridan. I'm so ashamed we did not!"

"Sir Tompkin, even if you had tried to rescue me, I could never have left my father. Nor can I still," I said.

He tucked away his handkerchief and patted my arm. "You are loyal and brave. And in spite of Wilhemina's worst efforts, we are together again at long last." Then he seemed to take a truly good look at me and broke into a joyful smile. "And how grown-up and beautiful you've become! Why, Prince Geoffrey seemed quite head over heels for you. Perhaps you'll be the next queen of Angland!"

"I'm afraid not," I said wryly. "I have no desire to be queen."

He looked somewhat taken aback, then said, "Indeed. Entirely up to you, of course, entirely, er... Now, what was I saying? Oh yes. It appears plain that your noble father Barnaby is most unwell. He will require nursing and excellent physicians. Lord Bluehart and I will see to it."

I had not felt such happiness in a very long time. "Oh, yes! It's just what I've been hoping for!"

"And it shall come to pass! But first we must concentrate upon dealing with your stepmother. We cannot obtain help for Barnaby if she blocks our efforts. As his legal wife, she has the right to deny him treatment. So let us see what we can do to invalidate their marriage. Clearly, he was not in possession of his mental faculties when she rushed him to the altar."

"I cannot agree more." I clasped my hands to my breast. "Have you spoken with the Lord Chief Justice? He is the only one who could render their marriage invalid."

"Yes. Months ago, we entreated him to investigate and intervene on behalf of Lord Lancastyr. But that moldering misanthrope told us, 'The man is free to trade his old friends for new ones and marry beneath him if he wishes. The law does not permit us to intervene.'"

At this point, Swiss returned from the ballroom with a dish of dainties and a goblet of wine. He enthusiastically dumped the plate on my lap, and I grabbed the goblet just in time to prevent it from spilling.

"Your dinner as requested," he said in a friendly voice.

Sir Tompkin gave him a reproving look, but Swiss obviously paid no attention as he took up a protective position to one side of us.

"Have you noticed," Sir Tompkin whispered, "that Prince Charming's bodyguard fellow is quite an odd sort? I can't say much for his bold manners. Things must be very different in your cousin's lands."

"Indeed, you cannot imagine how different," I said. "Do you mind if I partake of what the, er, bodyguard brought?" I hadn't seen such delicious fare in a long time, and I was so famished that even my eagerness to make plans with my father's old friend was not as strong as my desire to eat.

I confined myself to taking small ladylike bites rather than wolfing down the quail's eggs, pear-gorgonzola-pecan tart, and lingonberry trifle, then turned to Sir Tompkin to take up our discussion again.

"Now, Rose, there is a topic of a highly delicate nature I must broach with you," he said. "Though I hesitate to frighten you, I feel you should know."

I was not sure how many more frightening things

I could contemplate at this point, and yet I said, "Perhaps I have more courage than you realize. Go on, Sir Tompkin."

"Lord Bluehart and I heard a dreadful rumor about your stepmother." He hesitated, then said, "Never mind, I have thought better of it. I will not trouble your pretty little head over the sordid details."

My pretty little head? I tried not to feel outrage, but failed. "Are you hinting that you believe Wilhemina may have killed her first husband?" I asked.

He keeled backward, then righted himself. "Why, yes! Great heavens, you heard the gossip, too? Oh, how wicked, how dreadful. However did you manage to live under the same roof with a suspected murderess? You must have been in constant fear!"

I stared at him in surprise. Yes, Wilhemina had always frightened me. Nonetheless, my reaction to her evil was not what Sir Tompkin obviously expected of a well-brought-up young lass. My stepmother had forced me to be cunning, stiffened my resolve, and turned Lady Rose into Cinderella.

I was not ashamed of that name. I was proud of it. "I learned from that fear, Sir Tompkin."

Sir Tompkin declared, "You are braver than I would have been in your place. Never mind, you are safe now. And Lord Bluehart and I are searching for compelling proof that Wilhemina indeed had a hand in her first husband's death. If we find it, the Lord Chief Justice will change his mind and start proceedings against her."

"I wish the proof were already found." I frowned in frustration.

At that very moment, a familiar deep voice sounded across the garden. "Tompkin! And dear little Lady Rose! At last I've found you!"

"Bluey!" I bounded up from the bench and threw myself into the wide-flung arms of the usually reserved Lord Bluehart. While he kissed the top of my head, Sir Tompkin berated him for disappearing at such an important time, and Swiss edged closer to us with an expression of canny interest.

"Oh hush, Tompkin, I am here now, am I not?" Lord Bluehart said at last, then held me at arm's length and, with an uncharacteristically big smile on his usually impassive face, declared: "Both of you— come with me! Out of the clear blue sky, an ally has appeared who wishes to make a confession to you, and you alone, Lady Rose. I predict we shall soon see an end to the despicable Wilhemina!"

With Swiss at my back and Sir Tompkin at my

side, I followed Lord Bluehart into the castle and down a long corridor. We soon arrived at one of the smaller parlors, where visitors were accustomed to waiting for meetings with lesser members of the court.

"Here," Lord Bluehart said, opening the door with a return of his customary solemn demeanor. "In the Zhinese parlor. Prepare to be astonished, Rose."

He did not exaggerate. I stepped inside, then halted in utter confusion.

For there, seated on the red cushion of a black lacquered sofa, in a sober gray "Sunday Best" dress, sat Wilhemina's loyal servant—Cook.

Yes. The domineering Cook, who'd made my life miserable with her endless demands and constant hectoring. What on earth could she be doing at Castle Wendyn, with a crumpled, hopeless air and reddened eyes? Amid the black and scarlet of the parlor, decorated with busy Zhinese vases and carved stone Foo dogs, she looked wan and completely out of place.

Then came another shock: Lancastyr Manor's faithful housekeeper, Mrs. Grigson, came flying toward me out of nowhere, arms outstretched as if to give me a hug. "Lady Rose!" Under the disapproving stare of Lord Bluehart, she pulled back just before touching me and dropped a curtsy instead. "Oh my lady," she breathed. "Strange doings are afoot tonight! First this business with Cook, and now—we heard you've won Prince Geoffrey's heart!"

Then Pye came up next to Mrs. Grigson, keeping a respectful distance from the two titled gentlemen and Swiss. "You did it, Cinderella—I mean, Lady Rose!" he cried eagerly. "To blazes with Lady Wilhemina and that Miss Eustacia! You're the one who'll marry Prince Geoffrey, sure as sure!" he said.

"Pye? Mrs. Grigson?" I gaped in disbelief. "What is happening? What brings you here to the castle—and with Cook, of all people?"

Mrs. Grigson leaned in closer to me. "After seeing what that vile Lady Wilhemina did to you and your beautiful dress tonight, my patience was at an end. After I packed my bag, I hired a cab to come here with Pye."

I was still at sea. "But why?"

"Because I thought your father's dearest friends must be in attendance, even though they're bachelors with no daughters to marry off to the prince. They never miss a party at the castle, not them!"

Sir Tompkin flushed scarlet.

Now Mrs. Grigson's face grew hard and her usually placid eyes narrowed with anger. "I meant to find Sir Tompkin and Lord Bluehart, tell them everything, and beg them to rescue you and your father. I would even take my case to good King Tumtry himself, if I had to! Then, if you can believe it, just as Pye and I were leaving Lancastyr Manor, who should ask to join us but Mabel Hoovey—that is, Cook? I was that surprised, I almost had a spasm."

I felt I might be getting a spasm myself, at any minute.

Mrs. Grigson went on, "Cook had overheard where we were going and insisted she had a confession to make to your parents' friends. But when we arrived and she found out you had somehow made it to the ball after all—which I hope you'll explain sometime, my lady, we were flabbergasted when we found out—Cook insisted she would make the confession only to you."

I looked to the trembling Cook in wonderment.

Now Lord Bluehart cleared his throat and addressed Mrs. Grigson. "Good woman, you and the boy Pye have shown true loyalty tonight, coming here so boldly and arguing your way past the guards and the majordomo. Thank heaven they decided your cause was worthy and agreed to fetch me to speak with you. That is why you could not find me earlier, Tompkin," he said. "After you left the dancing to, er, refresh yourself, and I could not find you again, the majordomo located me and put me in charge of the situation."

Pye piped up, "Cinderella, he gave me and Mrs. Grigson three gold pieces—each! He said it was our back wages, because Lady Wilhemina never paid us."

Lord Bluehart gave a slight, tolerant smile. "Think of it as a measure of my deepest appreciation for your actions on behalf of Lady Rose."

Suddenly, Swiss erupted like a volcano. "We have a saying in my realm!" he shouted. "'No bake, flat cake!'"

We all jumped. Mrs. Grigson squealed.

"Eh?" Lord Bluehart lifted his monocle to his eye. "Most extraordinary! Whatever do you mean, my good man?"

"I mean, here you stand chattering about appreciation and gold pieces, while the crux of the matter sits before you—Mrs. Hoovey, the cook. What is it that she wants to confess? Question her now, or in the name of the great prince of the Northern Realm, I will do it for you!"

"I find you impolite in the extreme!" Lord Bluehart bridled, while at the same time Sir Tompkin said, "Don't you speak to Bluey like that!"

"Too bad," Swiss retorted. "We have another saying in my realm—"

"Spare us any more of your homegrown sayings, good sir!" Lord Bluehart put out a pale hand. "We are getting to that. And I believe the right to question this Cook belongs to Lady Rose."

Hiding the excitement and apprehension I felt inside, and regretting having eaten so many quail's eggs, I crossed the room and took a seat beside Cook. Pye and Mrs. Grigson gathered near us. Cook shied away as if afraid of being struck.

"Oh, Cook!" I said in surprise. "You have nothing to fear from me."

At this, she dropped her head in her hands and wailed, "My lady! I should have something to fear, that's the plain truth. I deserve punishment for what I've done. And so does *she*. Lady Wilhemina."

"Please tell us what you mean?"

Cook was not quite ready to answer so directly. "I've had this on my conscience for a powerful long time . . . but I justified it, Lady Rose. I believed what Wilhemina Draper told me. Then this evening, when I saw the cruel thing she did to you—and not just that, but a mountain of other things she did, fooling your pa, Lord Lancastyr, frittering away his money—I realized I had to tell you that she is a liar. She lied to me about you, and she lied about my former master—her husband, Mr. Jedrim Draper." She paused to draw in a shuddering breath.

Lord Bluehart stepped forward. "Perhaps this tale is not fit for your sweet girlish ears to hear," he said to me.

I held up a hand. "Thank you, my lord, but on the contrary: I am no longer a girl, and I must hear it to the end. Please go on, Cook—I mean, Mrs. Hoovey. What lies did my stepmother tell you?"

Cook kept her gaze downcast. "She told me her husband was a cruel monster who beat her. She claimed she had to leave him to save her life, and her daughters' lives, too."

"Is it true?" I asked.

"I thought it was, back then. Mr. Draper often wondered aloud about how his poor wife seemed always to be bruising and burning herself and coming up with black eyes. I thought at the time he was a beast who had done those things to her himself. I know different now! Mr. Draper was a kind man who wouldn't beat a drum, much less a woman, may he rest in peace."

Cook took a deep breath, then whispered, "Wilhemina told me Mr. Draper planned to beat her to death. She asked if I would save her life by taking his. So 'twas I, Wilhemina's most loyal servant, who carried out the evil deed on her behalf." She looked up and met my horrified gaze. "With rat poison."

Prince Char

Searching for Lady Apricot in the landscaped grounds of the castle, I wished I still had a rat's acute senses. I passed couples who stared at each other in lovestruck silence or chatted flirtatiously on the many stone benches scattered through the greenery. One of the amorous men had removed his sword belt and hooked it most negligently over the back of a bench, the better to hold his beloved's hand.

Mine, I think. The poor fellow didn't even notice when I used my marvelous opposable thumb and forefinger to lift his weapon. Chuckling to myself, I strapped it on as I strode down the path.

Suddenly, a strange feeling welled up in my chest. It was a bit like the sensation one gets when one has eaten a venomous lizard on an empty stomach. A type of soreness. It dawned on me that this was somehow connected to my taking of the sword.

Good gravy, I had heard of this! It was a human feeling.

Guilt.

Damnation. Should I return the lout's blade? Nay, I needed it for a most noble cause—protecting my lady. Taking what I require for the greater good is my royal prerogative.

Be that as it may, the confounded pain inside me was distracting. After a short deliberation, I made a mental note to give the thing back when it had served its purpose.

The instant I reached this decision, the guilt disappeared.

Being human was complicated indeed.

Keep to the task at hand, I told myself and walked on, peering into the darkness. Ahead was a deserted gazebo. It had three shallow steps leading up to a roofed octagonal platform.

This gave me an idea. Why not try the limits of these peculiar long legs? I ran forward and jumped. Whoosh! I sailed right up over the steps and onto the platform. In fact, I had underestimated my power and overshot, so I stumbled a little when I landed. "Huzzah!" I exclaimed, throwing my human arms up in jubilation. I hopped off the platform, backed up, and did it again.

I would have done it once more, had I not heard a voice address me in the language of the rats. "Is that Char? What are you doing?" It was Lady Apricot. She and her handmaidens had emerged from the bushes and come after me into the gazebo. I turned in their direction.

My mother took one good look at my new form, and her fur sprang out in spikes.

"My son! My poor, poor son, what a dreadful calamity!" she wailed, and her ladies echoed her. "A human! A human, alas, alack the day!"

I replied to her in the human tongue. "Stop, Mother, I haven't the time. I will resume my normal form at midnight." *Unless I can figure out a way to stop it.* "What are you doing here?"

This seemed to calm her somewhat. "Corncob and those Beef brothers told me what happened. I could scarce believe my ears. Neither could Pudding or Lambchop." She waved a tail at her handmaidens. "We came *immediately.* And that disgraceful Princess Mozzarella did nothing to help except give us a little gray rat as our guide, who scampered off once he got us to the ballroom. Why, Mozzarella ought to have sent an army along with me, for I am here to rescue you!"

"How exactly do you plan to accomplish this?"

"I will think of something!"

"Lady Mother, though I appreciate your sentiments, I have no need of rescue. In fact, I shall be frank with you: The case is quite the opposite. Had I any say in the matter, I would do my utmost to remain human."

"Remain . . . human?"

"Forever."

My mother turned up her snout and fell backward into her attendants' arms.

"My lady! My lady!" they cried.

I felt sorry for her. However, at twelve o'clock, when my dreams came to naught and I showed up as a rat again, my mother would soon forget her hysterics.

On the other hand, I could never forget Rose.

"Lady Lambchop; Lady Pudding." I addressed her attendants as they fussed over her. "Stay out of sight and keep my mother out of trouble, if you please. And by the way, she hasn't really fainted. Look at her tail—it's straight as a peppermint stick."

Lady Apricot hopped up. "You ungrateful wretch!

See if I try to rescue you ever again! I saw you with that Cinderella back in the rose garden! I warned she would bewitch you, and so she has!"

I knelt on the dusty boards of the gazebo floor. "Mother, may I hold you?"

She nodded with a small sniff.

I picked her up and cradled her in my arms. Then we touched, snout to nose.

"You no longer love me," she whimpered.

"I love you as much as ever I did," I said. "But every nestling must leave the nest. Though you've complained about my bachelorhood, still it has meant I stayed by your side for quite a long time. You've never shared me with another, except Swiss, though I'm not sure if he qualifies."

A tear trickled from the corner of her eye. "It's Cinderella, isn't it? You're abandoning me for Cinderella."

"I will not abandon you. But, yes, I am in love with Lady Rose. And if I return to being a rat, I can never, ever win her."

"Very well, my cherished son," she said after some time. "If you can contrive to stay with Cinderella and win her heart and hand, I will give my consent, although I cannot imagine how she could not love you. You are perfect in every way. Much better than any of those human men she has met."

"Dear Mother, it pains me to admit our conversation is to no purpose. You have seen me grow to an adult, persisting in the face of every challenge, allowing nothing to stand between me and a worthy goal. I see now that Lady Rose is the worthiest goal of all, and she will remain forever just beyond my reach. For once in my life, I must acknowledge defeat before I even begin. The best I can do in my few remaining hours as a man is to fulfill my mission to keep her and my people safe. Please be on hand when I change back, Mother. I will need you then."

Without considering what I was doing, I pressed my lips to the top of her head.

"Why, Char!" she exclaimed. "You truly have become human! You kissed me."

"Yes, Mother, though I have long wondered about the true significance of the human kiss."

"Surely you must have figured it out. The humans do it to show love."

"Yes, but parents and children, friends, and people who fall in love all kiss each other in ways that are, well, different. I have wanted to kiss Rose, but I fear she might misinterpret it as a rat trying to chew upon her face."

"Don't be silly, my son. There are as many different kinds of kisses as there are types of affection. When the time comes to demonstrate your love in that way, never fear: The feeling in your heart will guide you to do just as you ought." She paused a beat. "Do not despair, Char. There is magic afoot tonight. The goddess of the Lancastyr ring has set these events in motion, and it's not for us to say how they will end."

Sweet words. A parent's fond imaginings. "I must get back to Rose and Swiss. They're busy trying to save the Lancastyrs and destroy Wilhemina."

"Then why are you sitting here talking with me in the gardens? Put me down and be off with you," she said, unsuccessfully trying to hide a snuffle.

Good gravy, she was right! It must be getting late, and I still had not laid the trap I planned to set for Wilhemina.

I hastened away, leaving my mother to her handmaidens and her private tears.

When I returned to the flower garden, Rose, Swiss, and Sir Tompkin were gone. I hurried back to the courtyard where the fountain was, only to find that the crush of people who'd been gathered there when I left was now pressing rapidly back into the ballroom, as if something of great interest were happening within.

Oh, no. I had tarried too long. What was going on?

Cursing, I pushed forward and ran smack into the broad, medal-pinned chest of Lord Hamp. There was a panicked expression on his face.

"His Majesty King Tumtry requests that you join him in the ballroom at once! We have a ... delicate situation."

I required no further urging.

CINDERELLA

After Cook uttered her confession, we sat in silence until I asked, "Why did Wilhemina want her poor husband dead?"

Cook grimaced, then replied, "Wilhemina Draper was itching to come to the city and join her fine friend Harriet, who married one o' them baronets. Harriet had started to come visit in jewels and a costly coach, lording it over all the village women, and my mistress was jealous. Mr. Draper was a wealthy merchant, but he weren't wealthy enough for the mistress, no ma'am, and when she asked him to move the family business to the city of Glassevale, so she could live high alongside o' her friend, he flat-out said no."

Lord Bluehart interjected, "When this poor fellow Draper said no to Wilhemina's request, he was signing his own death warrant, was he not, Mrs. Hoovey? Wilhemina would not let a mere thing like a husband stand in the way of her ambition. She devised a scheme to murder him and use his money to move to the city, where she could find a wealthier husband."

"I realize that now," Cook said.

Then Swiss snarled, "And the rat poison you use with such a free hand around Lancastyr Manor these days? What about that, Mrs. Hoovey?"

Cook drew back in surprise. "What? Lady Wilhemina said there were far too many rats at the manor. She asked me to keep plenty of poison at hand and to leave choice morsels of fresh food for bait. We killed several rats before they got wise and stopped eating the poisoned victuals. Funny things, those rats. I know they're just dumb beasts, but it's almost as if they figured it out."

Swiss appeared unable to summon a response to this.

"So you had no plan to poison my father?" I asked.

Cook jumped up from the sofa. "My lady?"

"Answer the question!" rapped out Lord Bluehart. "Did you have designs on my old friend's life?"

"No! Never! Why would I poison Lord Lancastyr? He's a kind man, even if he's wandering in his wits, begging your pardon, my lady."

I believed her, but I had to press her further. "Did it not occur to you, Mrs. Hoovey, that poison worked once for my stepmother and that she might use it again? She has spent nearly every groat of my father's money, and she no doubt has plans to move on to another husband once the Lancastyr cupboard is bare. And that is why I sit by the cinders of the kitchen fireplace, doing your bidding without complaint. I have watched your every move, to protect my father. My wits are as good as yours, no matter how pretty and hapless I might appear."

All three of the servants gasped.

Then Mrs. Hoovey began to sob. "I have been a mean, bad-tempered old soul in the kitchen, stewing in my guilt and taking out my ill feelings on you, Cinderella—I mean, Lady Rose. And though I thought it was justice to kill Master Draper at the time, for I believed he threatened my mistress's life, I am also a murderess. They will hang me, but I declare, it's almost a relief."

Mrs. Grigson reached out and placed a sympathetic hand upon Cook's shoulder, which made her cry all the louder.

I pitied her.

"You shall not hang." I rose from the sofa and took off my emerald necklace. Then I gave the delicate gold links a savage twist at one end, to release a single glittering stone. It would garner a tidy sum if it were sold. I handed it to the dumbfounded Mrs. Hoovey.

"Take this gem and walk free," I said, crossing the floor and flinging wide the parlor door. "Go far away, and find somewhere to start afresh. Fear no pursuit, for my friends and I will not ask the Lord Chief Justice to charge you with this crime."

I ignored the chorus of protests and cries that immediately resulted, and turned to Swiss. "Now you know the truth," I said. "What do you think my kinsman Prince Charming would say?" Unspoken between Swiss and me was the knowledge of the rats Cook had killed in Lancastyr Manor.

"You have tempered judgment with mercy," he replied. "The prince would not object to your decision. The fault is your stepmother's. Let this pathetic creature Cook make her own way in the world."

After a whispered conference with Sir Tompkin, Lord Bluehart announced, "I cannot say we approve, but we shall abide by your decision. Just as soon as Cook writes out and signs her confession, with all the necessary dates and verifying details for the Lord Chief Justice, we shall escort her to a carriage. I shall call for pen, ink, and parchment."

Sir Tompkin said, "The Lancastyrs are saved!"

A subdued little cheer went up in the room.

"Swiss," I said. "Where is Prince Charming?"

PRINCE CHAR

The panicked Lord Hamp and I made our way with difficulty through the crowd in the main ballroom. There was shock, fear, and a hum of scandal in the air. Though I could not yet see him, I could hear Prince Geoffrey shouting.

"Who is the villainness spreading this vile slander?" he thundered. "Come out, whoever you are! I will have your head! Don't dare to hide from me!"

Double damnation. I wondered what hapless person had riled up the crazy prince this time. If Geoffrey caused a scene now, it might destroy my scheme of focusing his murderous attention this evening upon one particular target.

"He must be stopped," Lord Hamp said as we

fought our way toward the throne. "There is a brotherhood among royalty, Your Highness. Help King Tumtry so that Angland does not fall apart. You said you came in friendship."

"I certainly did. But what do you expect me to do? Your prince is unfit to rule. I have heard about the murder of Quintilius Porter, and I will not help you continue to lie about Geoffrey's sanity so that you may rivet him to some poor unsuspecting female."

A look of despair washed over Lord Hamp's strong features. He suddenly had the air of a man twenty years older. "It was the only plan we could devise. There has never been a break in the succession, since the days of the founding of the realm. When King Tumtry dies, if Prince Geoffrey has not married a steady girl to mitigate the effects of his madness and give birth to an heir, the people will soon depose him, and a fight for the crown will ensue."

I could no longer hold back. "Then set Geoffrey aside and arrange a contest of valor and intelligence to win the rulership, as we do in my realm!"

"The king is considering it," Hamp said with a look I could not identify.

We were much closer to the throne now. I could see Geoffrey's face, suffused with purple rage. He sprayed spittle as he continued to yell about the gossip he'd overheard. "Anyone with information about this slander must come forward!"

And this was Angland's heir to the throne?

Humans!

I swallowed my impatience. "Is it true that King Tumtry is dying?"

"Lord Brimfield and I are of the firm belief he is still alive due only to his determination to see the future of his people safely settled. I do not know how much longer he can hold on."

So I wasn't the only one on borrowed time tonight.

We pushed past the last of the guests, emerging into the space around the throne. King Tumtry was slumped over, with the air of one who has already given up. Lord Brimfield was remonstrating with Geoffrey from a safe distance. Prince Geoffrey was holding aloft his sharp, bright sword.

My hand inched closer to the hilt of my own weapon.

"A moment for bold action, eh, Lord Hamp?" I said to him under my breath, and stepped forward.

"Hail, Geoffrey, my royal friend!" I greeted him heartily. "What's amiss? May I help in any way?"

He swung around. "Yes!" he cried. "You, of all people, will wish to be part of this. You cannot guess, Prince Charming, what sordid rumor has come to my ears. It is about your very own kinswoman and my future bride, Rose de Lancastyr."

"Indeed?" I came forward and clapped him on the shoulder. "How grateful I am that you care so greatly for Lady Rose's reputation. Oops." I feigned an awkwardness around the point of his sword. "Er, do you mind sheathing that for a moment, Cousin? You don't take it amiss that I call you *Cousin*, do you? After all, we soon will be family, is that not so? For I can see how you feel about Lady Rose."

"Yes, yes." He had the air almost of a bull who has seen too many dangling red flags. His hands were practiced and deadly steady, though, as he slid the sword back into its scabbard with a metallic hiss.

Good.

Lord Hamp gave me a look of gratitude. He now moved to the side of King Tumtry, who was leaning forward in a new attitude of tension, which I considered better than the hopelessness I'd seen in him not a minute before.

"Come," I said to Prince Geoffrey. "Instruct me."

It was unbelievable. He did. Geoffrey confided to me (and to everyone else who was listening), "It has come to my attention that a woman here tonight is smearing Lady Rose's character. The perfidious slanderer—whoever she is—said that since the death of Lady Jane, your cousin Rose has lost her wits."

Oh, the blessed irony. "Nonsense," I growled.

"Ah." Prince Geoffrey nodded. "So the gossip angers you, too!"

"Yes, it does." It also thrilled me. For I knew who had dreamed up this falsehood. She'd betrayed herself right into my hands.

Geoffrey did not notice my rush of cold joy. He continued filling me in on his thoughts, "Prince Charming, I did not see the speaker who spread the lies. But I shall find her. If I must kill everyone in this room one by one, I will stop the treasonous gossip about my soon-to-be bride! You will help, will you not?"

It had come—the moment for which I'd been made a man. I would fulfill my charge, my duty as ruler. And yet I would not literally break my promise to Lady Rose. Pretty neatly plotted, eh?

"I shall do more than help, Prince Geoffrey. I am

privy to the information you seek." I raised my voice and called, "Wilhemina Draper, who styles herself Lady Lancastyr, come forward! Come reap the harvest you have sown!"

The revelation spread through the crowd like blood through water. I heard a scream and someone crying.

Lord Brimfield crept up to me. "Noble prince, are you sure of what you're doing?" he nervously mumbled.

"Perfectly. I am restoring the House of Lancastyr, and taking care of a particularly nasty criminal as well. Watch and see how it is done."

During this exchange, the people of Glassevale accomplished the unpleasant task of seizing Wilhemina and delivering her up to face the prince's rough justice. In short order, she landed at Prince Geoffrey's feet. Her stiffly curled hair had come loose from its pins and her red tiara was missing.

"Aha! The guilty one! Thank you, royal cousin." Geoffrey favored me with a comely smile. "I am in your debt. And to think that earlier tonight I considered having you assassinated!"

"My prince!" Lord Brimfield exclaimed in horror.

I was almost shocked into a laugh.

Then Geoffrey turned on Wilhemina. "Wretched

creature! What have you to say for yourself? Is there any reason why I should not strike your head from your body this instant?"

Then, suddenly, came the cry of a child: "Release her!"

The crowd fell back to reveal a frantic Jessamyn, pulling Lord Lancastyr along by the hand. Eustacia was behind them, her zucchini-green gown looking as if she'd been drawn through a bramble hedge rather than a press of people.

"Your Highness, please—spare my mother!" Jessamyn begged.

Wilhemina, on her knees before the prince, seemed to jerk out of her stunned state when she heard her daughter's voice. "Your Highness, most benevolent prince! I am wrongfully accused. I have done nothing! Do not take my head," she rasped.

I should have been reveling in this moment, watching my people's enemy pleading for her life.

I wasn't.

In fact, that pit-of-the-stomach feeling—guilt—was starting up again.

Geoffrey turned to Eustacia. "Are you her daughter, too?" he asked in a dangerously musical tone of voice.

Eustacia hesitated, seeming all at once to realize the peril she was in, standing there next to her mother. She shook her head till the corkscrew curls swung out wide. Then she stepped backward into the throng and disappeared.

A real rock of loyalty, that one.

"I am her daughter!" little Jessamyn declared, strong and clear. "And this is her husband, Barnaby de Lancastyr. And *you* are nothing but a big bully. You need to let my mamma go right now!"

Zounds! Was this the fearful child who'd shrieked when she'd seen rats in the attic only a short time ago?

"Stepfather," Jessamyn said, tugging at Lord Lancastyr's long silk tunic. "Do something. Save my mother!"

Lord Lancastyr stood indecisively by, looking at the vivid little girl with a bemused expression. "What's the to-do about?" he asked. Then he squinted toward the throne. "Why, is that you up there, King Tumtry? I say, queer goings-on tonight!"

King Tumtry made no move. He seemed to have decided, as had his councillors, to leave this all up to me.

I swiftly took charge of the two innocents. "Lord

Lancastyr, Jessamyn—come along with me. You don't belong here."

"Hold, Prince Charming!" Geoffrey said. "I have a question to ask of the daughter. Little girl, have you ever heard this woman"—he tossed a careless hand in Wilhemina's direction—"abuse or spread lies about your stepsister, Rose de Lancastyr? Upon your oath, speak the truth!"

This was an unforgivable position in which to place a child, particularly Wilhemina's child.

Jessamyn's lower lip began to tremble. "I—I— would rather not say."

Wilhemina tried to rise from her knees, and Prince Geoffrey pushed her back down. Her heavy scarlet skirts pooled around her on the floor like blood. "Stay," he ordered, "while I decide your fate."

Wilhemina next tried to defend herself, to forestall any revelations Jessamyn might make, her voice thinning with terror. "Your Highness, what lady has not spoken harshly to members of her household now and again?"

Prince Geoffrey ignored her. "Little girl," he said to Jessamyn once more, "did your mother ever say Rose de Lancastyr has aught amiss with her wits?"

Jessamyn broke down and sobbed. "She did, yes!

Oh, Mamma, you ought not to have done so many terrible things to Rose. Now look what has happened. You can be so cruel at times, Mamma, but I don't want you to die!"

With a satisfied smile, Geoffrey drew his sword.

CINDERELLA

Swiss and I, possessed by a shared premonition of doom, hurried from the Zhinese parlor, leaving the others to take care of Cook's written confession. As we passed a fireplace, I noted with wild despair that the clock on the mantel read eleven-thirty.

"Whiskers and wedding cakes!" Swiss exclaimed. "That can't be the right time! Only one half hour left before the spell dissolves."

Char had only a half hour left to be human?

I could not fathom how the minutes had slipped through our fingers already, or how I'd lost track of my beloved Rat Prince. I'd accomplished much tonight, yet in the matter of finding a future for me and Char together, there was simply nothing to be done. But at the very least, I wanted to spend every remaining second by his side.

I picked up my skirts and ran down the wide red-carpeted corridor. The glass slippers lent speed to my feet, yet Swiss kept pace with me easily.

When we burst into the ballroom, it was packed with people. Yet they were all perfectly, unnaturally still. My heart rose to my throat.

"Uh-oh," Swiss said, moving into a defensive posture in front of me.

My gaze swept past him and over the heads of the crowd, drawn to a group standing by King Tumtry's throne. They were quite familiar figures. "Oh no."

Char stood straight and tall beside Prince Geoffrey. My father slouched off to the side of the throne, disconnected from the proceedings. And there was my darling Jessamyn, her mouth wide open in a scream she seemed too terrified to utter.

My stepmother was on her knees in front of Prince Geoffrey. As I watched, he brandished his large sword high in the air.

There were gasps and cries from the crowd.

No, oh no. Char. *Char!*

Just as Geoffrey's sword was about to complete its downward arc, faster than my eyes could follow, there was a loud clang of sword falling upon sword, rather than the swoosh and clunk of a woman parting with her head.

And Char was there, holding a blade of his own, staring into Geoffrey's astonished face.

"It's awkward, Your Highness," Char said. "Killing the ball guests. Puts a bit of a damper on the dancing."

He had done it. He'd saved Wilhemina.

"Prince Charming!" Jessamyn bawled. "Thank you! Thank you!" She moved closer to my father, who put a hand on her shoulder.

Wilhemina scrambled up from the floor and tried to run away. A pair of palace guards caught and held her.

This was not yet over. Char's weapon was still locked with Geoffrey's.

Swiss leaned toward me, anguish on his face. "Geoffrey is an accomplished swordsman," he whispered. "How will Char, who has never in his life held a sword till now, defeat him?"

Panic gripped me. "Go to him! Protect him if need be!"

We both began to push desperately forward.

"King Tumtry must put a stop to this!" I cried to

Swiss. "And why on earth was Geoffrey about to kill Wilhemina?"

"Geoffrey is either mad or bad, my lady," Swiss informed me. "Perhaps a bit of both."

I heard a bellow like a raging beast, and the ring of jarring steel.

"Let me through," I pleaded with the phalanx of people. "Oh, make way, I must reach my beloved prince!" *Char, Char, Char.*

When people saw who I was they allowed me to pass, no doubt thinking the prince I spoke of was Geoffrey. Swiss and I broke free of the crowd just in time to see Geoffrey aim a mighty hack at Char's head.

Char nimbly swerved, avoiding the blow. Then he paused and gave a pleased smile, as if surprised at his own maneuver. Of course he would be surprised. He had only had a human body for a matter of hours. *Do not let yourself be distracted! Have a care!*

Geoffrey rushed at him again, and Char leapt atop the low platform that held the throne, still wearing the same expression of delight. Geoffrey said in an infuriated voice, "I will slice that smirk off your lips!"

They were getting dangerously close to my stepsister and my father. "We must move them to safety," I urged Swiss, nodding in their direction. We dashed over and drew Jessamyn and my father nearer to the second set of guards who stood behind the king's seat. There, I took Jessamyn into my arms.

"Oh dear one!" I cried.

"Sister!" she murmured brokenly, burying her face in my bosom. "Where have you been? Take pity on my mother, Rose, though she's been most wicked. Save her life!"

"You and Prince Charming have already saved it, my darling." I kissed her head.

Geoffrey was still threatening Char, as they now circled each other. "I will cut your pretty face to ribbons, sir," he said, with an ugly curl to his mouth.

Char seemed hardly to notice. "Thank you for the compliment about my face. I can't take any credit for it. By the way, I can see why you enjoy using your sword so much, Your Highness," he said, cutting a careless Z shape into the air. "Really, most diverting—hey!"

Geoffrey had taken a swipe at him, which he narrowly avoided by arching his back and jumping onto his toes.

It was a move as graceful as any I had seen

performed in a ballet. Good heavens, were Prince Geoffrey not in such deadly earnest, Char would have been a joy to watch.

Swiss's fascinated whisper met my ear: "Look at that. And to think I worried about him. I should have known better."

"Stop dancing about and fight!" Geoffrey taunted.

Char laughed outright at this sally. "I thought you loved to dance. But if you insist . . ."

Whip-whip-whip-whip-whip!

He engaged the very tip of Geoffrey's sword with his own, back and forth, so quickly that Geoffrey stumbled and almost fell.

Char stood by politely and gave him time to recover. His fine black hair tumbled over his forehead, and he tossed it back. Yes, he was enjoying this, much in the manner of an athletic contest.

"Kill him now and be done with it!" Swiss yelled, making me hop several inches in startlement and let go of Jessamyn.

Char did not take his brilliant gaze from his opponent, though he, too, must have been startled to hear Swiss. "There is a brotherhood among royalty," he declared. "Prince Geoffrey shall have his chance. Your Highness," he called, "let us cease these hostilities. Grant Lady Wilhemina her life, and I will stand down. Lady Rose shall determine a proper punishment for her stepmother."

Geoffrey recovered and raised his weapon. "Nay. The stepmother will die because it pleases me, and so will you." He leapt forward with a practiced, masterful thrust, which Char parried.

"I will die someday, but not at your pleasure and not at your hands," Char replied, flicking his sword swiftly at Geoffrey and neatly cutting the clasp from his velvet cape. The expression Geoffrey wore as his cape fell from his shoulders was a stupefied blank.

The gathered onlookers gave an *Oooh* of admiration. I surveyed their faces. They didn't seem frightened anymore; they were excited.

Maddened by this evidence that his own noble peers were on Char's side, not his, Geoffrey roared and came at my beloved again. Char held him off. To and fro, to and fro they went.

"Lady Rose," Swiss breathed, fear in his voice. "The time. Look at the time!" He pointed to a clock face embedded in the wooden paneling of the orchestra gallery.

No. *No!*

"My love!" I cried, agony in my voice that only

Char and Swiss could understand. "It is one quarter to the hour of midnight!"

Char's face lost its insouciance. His black brows snapped together and the clean line of his jaw grew hard. The next move he took was swifter than we onlookers could track. One moment Geoffrey was thrusting at Char again with a flourish deft in its delivery; the next, Geoffrey's sword went spinning off in the air to land with a clank and a sort of whistle as it slid across the marble floor.

Geoffrey lay on his back before the king's throne, and Char stood with one foot on his chest, the tip of his blade at Geoffrey's throat.

He would kill the vanquished Prince Geoffrey now, I had no doubt. The Rat Prince would save the kingdom of Angland in his own way. He had won the right to do so. I stood ready to cover Jessamyn's face with my hands, to shield her from the sight.

But Char's dark gaze found mine and held.

"Yield or die," he said to Geoffrey.

A deafening cheer rose from the crowd.

Prince Char

Geoffrey yielded.

I stepped away from him and sheathed my sword.

Finally, King Tumtry decided to intervene. He struggled to his feet. "Guards, take my son and bind his hands," he commanded.

Though his voice was not strong, it carried, and his subjects politely went wild as three strapping fellows overwhelmed the shouting Geoffrey and carried him off to stand beside Wilhemina. Not surprisingly, she shied away from him, but she wisely kept her mouth clamped shut.

If the guards had been so well able to handle the belligerent prince this whole time, why had King Tumtry not given his order before? He could have saved me the trouble and his son the humiliation of being defeated at the point of my steel.

Not that it had been much trouble. What an opportunity to flex this human physique to its fascinating, invigorating limits! I wouldn't mind doing it again . . . but of course I never would.

As Geoffrey began to hurl insults and accusations at his father, at me, and at everyone else in the vicinity, the king ordered, with sadness behind his stern tone, "Bind his mouth, too."

"Char!" Now Lady Rose, the delight of my eyes and the deepest wish of my soul, came running to me. I caught her in my arms, whirled her in the air—*the final time I will have these arms with which to hold her*—and at last, I covered her lips with mine.

So. This was what a kiss really meant.

Tumult arose in the ballroom. People were shouting our names—"Prince Charming! Rose de Lancastyr!"

She responded to my kiss with enthusiasm, then pulled away to look into my eyes. "Char, my love. This cannot be the end. How can fate be so cruel as to give us only a handful of hours together?"

"It was Ashiira who gave us those hours, and I would not trade them for the entire rest of my existence. How the goddess must love the house of Lancastyr, to bless both humans and rats with her magic. We've forged an understanding between our families that will last for another five hundred years."

I was trying hard to lift her spirits.

She was having none of it. Nor was I, for that matter.

But I had no room for regret. I was too busy reveling in her heady, clear scent. The sweetness of her spirit. The poetry of her face, her hair, the slope of her delicate shoulders, the flawless sweep of her neck, the tiny nip of her waist—I scanned her again and again, trying to burn upon my memory how Char the man felt about Rose the woman, before she was lost to me.

Despair was in her next words. "How can I live without you?"

I started to soothe her. "Cherished one, don't forget Lancastyr Manor is my ancestral home. I shall always be there, as I was before, watching over you and caring for you . . ."

No.

I realized as I said it that I could no longer live as a rat in Lancastyr Manor and subject us both to the resulting daily agony of longing and hopelessness.

I would have to leave my home and my princedom. When I disappeared, the rats of the Northern Rat Realm would hold a trial to find a new prince, and assuredly, this time Swiss would win. He would be a fine ruler. Meanwhile, I would find my path in another realm, perhaps even another city. Or take up residence in a stone wall in a pasture far, far away.

"You will leave," she said flatly, seeing the decision in my eyes. "No, Char . . . no. There must be something we can do!"

Then Swiss was there, his familiar presence beckoning me back to what I once had been. "My prince," he said, "ten minutes more!"

"Go stand behind the throne, Swiss," I told him. "When the moment comes you may slip quietly away. Find my mother and her ladies as well as Truffle and the mice who were turned into horses, and see them safely home. And please see to it that the mice who sewed my lady's gown are rewarded for their part in tonight's doings."

"Why are you giving me these orders?" he asked. "We will do it together when you come back with us at midnight!"

I glanced at Rose. "I am not coming. I abdicate my throne, Swiss. Do your duty to the realm and rule until another prince is chosen, which will undoubtedly be you. That is my last command as your sovereign."

"What are you doing?" Swiss demanded. There was a quaver in his voice.

"I believe you already know, don't you, Swiss? You have been like a brother to me."

Swiss lay a hand on my shoulder. He was grimacing, in a losing battle to keep his human face a blank. "I do know. Goodbye, dear friend. And you need not stay away forever," he said. "Surely someday the hurt will heal and you can come see me?"

I didn't trust myself to speak.

Swiss said no more but squeezed my shoulder once before turning away and hastening to stand behind the throne as I bade him.

Then King Tumtry raised his hands in the air. "My people," he said. "Your attention, please."

The babble of the crowd died down.

"As I believe most of you are well aware," he continued, "my health is failing. Few days are left to me on this earth."

He waited for the ballgoers to settle down once more. I sympathized with him but was impatient, since my precious seconds as a human were racing by—seconds I would much rather have spent alone with Lady Rose. I contented myself instead with clinging to her hand and watching her expression as the king gave his speech.

"My privy councillors and I have been much exercised in our minds as to who should inherit my throne when I am gone," the king announced. "My son, Geoffrey, cannot rule, for he is not capable, as you have seen. My people, for this I apologize."

The guests murmured their understanding.

"Tonight, you have met Prince Charming of the Northern Realm." King Tumtry waved a hand at me.

Huh? Why drag me into this?

He went on. "A brilliant diplomat, a kind and wise ruler, a courageous champion of what is just and right. And a consummate swordsman!"

I felt this characterization was a bit too generous. Hang on—was I feeling *modesty*?

"He forgot to say *handsome*," Rose said before kissing my cheek, and the humans, inexplicably, cheered. Her green eyes shone with tears. "I love you so."

"And I love you," I breathed. "Forever. No matter which body it beats in, my heart shall always be yours."

Yet King Tumtry had not finished. "I have recently learned that in the Northern Realm where Prince Charming rules, the rulership is given not by birth, but by trial." He gave me a meaningful look. Well, at least he'd been paying attention earlier. "Only the most intelligent, the bravest, and the most compassionate man or woman in the land may rise to the throne."

I wasn't going to correct him in front of everyone, but compassion was not exactly one of the qualities rats look for in their potential prince or princess. A successful candidate for the rat throne must win all the fights and hand down the wisest judgments on legal disputes, and must also vanquish the others in a test of how much wine he or she can drink at one sitting and still keep a clear head. And then, there is the sausage-eating contest.

King Tumtry went on, "As soon as my royal councillors and I heard this intriguing idea, we knew it was the answer to our prayers for securing the succession of Angland. Lord Hamp, Lord Brimfield, and I arranged a test of our own tonight to determine who would rule this land when I am gone. We asked Prince Charming to attempt to master a situation crucial to the kingdom."

Hmmm.

"My loyal subjects, what you have just witnessed was the outcome of that test. Prince Charming prevailed with courage, wisdom, and calm. And he vanquished my son in a duel with great honor as well as skill, though Geoffrey's prowess with a sword has never before been bested. Prince Charming, ruler of the Northern Realm and now the next king of Angland, come forward!"

Me?

The king bent a warm, hopeful gaze my way. "If you will agree, tonight I shall lay aside my burden of rulership, and I will crown you king here before my assembled nobles, so that all may witness our kingdom is safe in your valiant hands."

The ballroom exploded into deafening acclaim.

"Huzzah, huzzah! Long live the future King Charming!"

King Tumtry boomed out, "And from now on, the heir to the rulership shall always be required to pass a test devised by the royal councillors before ascending the throne!"

I sent an incredulous glance toward Lord Hamp, then to Lord Brimfield, and finally to King Tumtry himself. There was confirmation in their grave smiles. I had not misheard.

"Char?" Rose said in a tremulous voice. Then, stronger, louder, "Char!"

I opened my mouth to speak—then it began.

The chimes of the clock in the tower outside, rever-berating through the walls of the palace.

Striking twelve.

Bong.

I took both my lady's hands. "Go to Jessamyn and your father," I said. "Stand by them. I would not humiliate you when my transformation takes place. The people will mock you afterward for falling in love with a rat."

She held my hands tighter and straightened her spine. "I shall remain with you. The last sight you will see as a man is me, loving you. And I am proud to love the Rat Prince who won the throne of An-gland as well as my heart."

She had the truest, bravest heart I'd ever known.

"Lady Rose, my Cinderella," I softly said, "if I had become a man forever, and this night were the begin-ning of many nights for the rest of our lives, would you have become my bride?"

"Yes," she said without hesitation.

Still the pitiless clock kept on striking.

My love, my love, my Rose. I counted seven . . . eight . . . nine . . .

CINDERELLA

Seven . . . eight . . . nine . . .

Every candle in the room went out at once. Before anyone could scream or run, a noise like a rushing waterfall cascaded over the ballroom. The air around us swirled with pale blue light. A crescendo of majestic, wild music blew past us, and suddenly . . .

"Tumtry of the house of Wendyn, King of Angland, you have chosen well. You have saved your domain."

The words echoed from wall to wall before the blue light took shape and approximated the form of a woman over ten feet tall, her hair a floating blue flame, her robe flowing water. Ashiira! She hovered in front of King Tumtry, who tottered and collapsed back onto his silver throne. His advisers bravely stepped up, Lord Hamp clutching the king's shoulder, the withered Lord Brimfield steadying himself against Lord Hamp.

I looked at Char. My love was still a man! Hope warred with disbelief within my breast. A quick glance about showed me that Swiss, too, remained in human form.

Had the clock struck twelve? I hadn't heard it.

Char put his arm around me and hugged me close. "Just see how Ashiira has put on an impressive form to frighten everyone," he murmured. "The minx."

"Did you just call the Lancastyr goddess a minx?"

He smiled. I noticed a dimple in one of his cheeks.

Ashiira spoke. "Come stand before me, Geoffrey of the house of Wendyn, sometime Prince of Angland." As she gave the summons, Geoffrey was propelled toward her. The bonds fell magically from his wrists and mouth before he came to a terrified stop.

How amazing that he could stand upright in her presence! Whatever else he was, Geoffrey was not a coward. I quickly looked to his father. The pain I saw there was too great; I had to shift my gaze away.

"Geoffrey, though your father believes you mad, it is not so. You have been given many chances to choose well, and you have chosen badly," Ashiira said, still in that powerful echoing voice so unlike the dulcet trill she used at Lancastyr Manor. "Your life ought to be forfeit for the good of the realm. However, out of consideration for your royal parent, I will not carry out that sentence. Another choice lies before you. Spend your days doing good works to atone for the misdeeds you have committed and the noble deeds you have never done—or be punished as I see fit."

"I am prince of this land," he shrieked, "whether my traitorous father acknowledges me or not. You cannot make and unmake a king, whoever you are!"

Ashiira's glowing lips formed a quarter-moon of a smile. "I am a divinity. I make and unmake kings." She pointed a burning blue finger at the clock above the musician's gallery. "I have taken us out of the normal passage of time to craft this moment from infinity. Now we shall return to the ebb and flow of your world, where the clock has tolled nine of the twelve strokes until midnight. Geoffrey de Wendyn, you have up to the last stroke to make your decision."

A shock rocked everyone slightly backward, as if the earth quaked. I saw it ripple through the gathering. Then in a panic, I heard the clock tower resume:

Bong.

Bong.

"Goodbye, my love," Char whispered. He dropped a kiss on my forehead. We clung to each other.

Bong . . . twelve.

Thousands of candles sprang back to life at once, and the room was flooded with light. Screams ripped the air. Shocked yells came from the crowd: "A rat! Did you see—he turned into a rat!"

"Char!" I gasped.

Joy—unutterable, unquenchable joy! For my love still stood within my embrace, whole and human, his eyes wide and bright, his slender frame vibrating with wonder.

"Rose, my heart!" He hugged me tight, then spun me around and pointed at the floor several paces away. "Behold!"

There, amid a heap of princely clothing, within a royal circlet of twisted gold, sat a golden-haired rat, hunched over, sniffing the air.

Ashiira declared sonorously, "Justice has been done. Balance is restored. Under the guidance of a noble and loyal breed of local rats, the former prince shall learn once more how to be human."

Suddenly Swiss appeared, in his rat form again, nipping at Geoffrey's new rat hindquarters and driving him toward the courtyard. I took this to mean that Swiss would be the one delivering Geoffrey's humanity lessons. Before disappearing into the night, he stopped and saluted in our direction.

Char and I waved back.

Then our attention was pulled to Ashiira, who was far from finished. "Justice shall also be done upon you, Wilhemina Draper, enemy of the house of Lancastyr," she proclaimed with flashing eyes to my stepmother, who'd been languishing in the grip of the palace guards.

"Good heavens, Char!" I exclaimed. "I forgot about Wilhemina!"

"So did I," he said. "If you'd told me earlier today that I could actually drop the blasted woman from my thoughts, even for a minute, I wouldn't have believed you."

"Would you have believed it if I told you King Tumtry would make you his heir?" I asked.

"I still don't believe that," he replied.

"Wilhemina Draper, you are a murderess," Ashiira proclaimed. Flames leapt about her forbidding, glorious countenance. "You wedded Barnaby de Lancastyr under false pretenses. You are not, and have never been, a Lancastyr."

Wilhemina's skin drained of color; her lips went gray.

"Mercy, great goddess!" a little voice quavered. It belonged to Jessamyn. "Mercy upon my mother, I beg!"

Oh, Jessamyn! My conscience smote me. Throughout this fearsome scene of judgment, the brave child had been alone, with only my father to lean upon.

Char and I both hurried toward her. Then we saw that Sir Tompkin and Lord Bluehart had gotten there first. Sir Tompkin was holding her hand, and Lord Bluehart stood staunchly by my father.

I thanked our dear friends as Char scooped Jessamyn up and held her, big as she was, upon his hip. Then he turned toward the goddess. "Ashiira," he said. "This child is a courageous and kind soul, a true sister to Lady Rose. Her wishes should be considered."

The goddess inclined her head.

"Rose," Jessamyn whispered as I kissed her brow. "Your handsome prince came after all. Do you think he will help Mamma?"

Sir Tompkin pulled out his big handkerchief.

My heart ached for Jessamyn, who I could see did not fully understand the accusations against her mother. Someday when she was older and strong enough to bear the burden, she would learn the truth of how Wilhemina had ordered Cook to kill her father. But not now.

"Goddess Ashiira," I said. "You have rightly declared that justice must be done upon Wilhemina. On behalf of the Lancastyrs, I request that you allow me to mete out her sentence myself."

The flames around Ashiira faded away. She turned to us, seeming now more like the fairy creature from the stable yard at Lancastyr Manor than an awesome bringer of divine judgment. "So be it, Lady Rose. This woman's life is in your hands."

It seemed everyone's gaze now turned to me, except Wilhemina's. Her eyes were squeezed shut; her bloodless lips moved restlessly, but no sound came out.

I hesitated a moment. "If it please Your Majesty King Tumtry," I said, "she will be confined in Castle Wendyn until we can arrange her transport to the Convent of the Order of the Silent Nuns. There, she will make up for her crimes by helping the poor, tilling the fields, weaving shrouds, and doing other good works, as Geoffrey might have done had he accepted the offer of the goddess. There is much more to be said for atonement than for punishment.

And by the way, Wilhemina," I said loudly and distinctly, "the Silent Nuns wear only hemp sandals and homespun brown robes."

Her eyes flew open. "Brown is not my color!" she shrieked.

Without further ado, the king said to his guards, "Lock her up in the dungeons."

Wilhemina protested. "But the dungeons are filthy. And there are *rats*!"

Char winked at me over the top of Jessamyn's curls. I concluded that he would take it upon himself to make sure Wilhemina's time in the dungeons with the rats would be most instructive, before she made it to the convent.

Then he cuddled my stepsister as Wilhemina was marched away. "Do you see? You saved your mamma's life, Jessamyn," he soothed. "All will be well."

For the first time since my own mother's death, I felt deep down inside that this was actually true.

Now Ashiira called, "Lady Rose and Prince Charming, please come forward."

Char let Jessamyn slide down to stand on her own again, and Sir Tompkin took charge of her. Then we walked together toward Ashiira, who still hovered over King Tumtry and his councillors. The king seemed strained and limp, but his councillors wore eager expressions, as if they could hardly believe the good fortune of this unexpected resolution to their worries.

Then the goddess looked kindly upon us.

"Prince Charming, you must choose. Do you wish to become ruler of this kingdom, or remain prince of the Northern Realm, which you have led so well for so long?"

His voice strong and sure, Char replied, "In my princedom there are good candidates and true for the throne. I have no qualms about relinquishing my duties."

She gave a gesture of understanding and approval, tracing a shimmering arc in the air with both hands and bringing them together again. "Then do you now accept the bounty and the charge of King Tumtry to become king of the Realm of the Angles, the Southern Hills, the Vales and Islands, and the Border Marches, as long as you shall yet live?"

Char said, "If I may share the rulership with my love, Rose de Lancastyr, as my queen."

I felt a shock of pure bliss. Char would be my husband, and I his wife.

"Are there any objections from King Tumtry or his people?" Ashiira asked.

A roar of approval rose from the packed ballroom as King Tumtry declared, "I am gratified and honored to accept your condition, Prince Charming."

"Then let it be!" Ashiira said. "Lady Rose and Prince Charming, you have both fought strong forces arrayed against you, and you have proven yourselves the stronger by far. My next words will give you to each other in marriage, and give your family—the Lancastyrs—unto the land of Angland in perpetuity as its sacred sovereigns, as long as you are fit to rule and your heirs pass the tests of worthiness. Do you accept?"

Char, irrepressible to the end, whispered to me, "Is this a trick question?"

"We accept!" I hastily responded.

King Tumtry beckoned Lord Brimfield to him. With utmost dignity, Lord Brimfield came up behind the king and lifted the big golden crown from his head. The jewels in it sparkled Lancastyr blue in the light Ashiira cast as he held it high. I marveled at this, for the stones had been red before, the color of the house of Wendyn.

"Kneel, both of you," Lord Brimfield said in a deep and carrying tone. "And be granted the crown of the kingdom."

Ashiira halted him a moment, and called Lord Hamp forward. "A crown is required also for the queen," she said. From a shower of light, a beautiful sapphire circlet glimmered into being before the astonished councillor. He reached up to pluck it from the air somewhat gingerly, as if afraid it might burn him.

Then together, Char and I each dropped down on one knee, and with ancient and sacred words, Lord Hamp and Lord Brimfield bestowed the throne of Angland upon us. I felt the weight of the crown settle gently upon my head.

Lord Hamp said, in throbbing tones, "Arise, King Charming and Queen Rose."

I felt Char's hand clasp mine.

The people—my people, and Char's—cheered again.

KING CHARMING

You would think my treasured queen and I had been vouchsafed everything we could ever have dreamed of. But there was something else.

"Great goddess," I said to Ashiira, "my thanks to you shall be undying. Yet I have one more boon to ask."

Kindness streamed from her face in a faint halo. "Dear King Charming, I know what you would ask of me, yet I must not give it."

She moved toward my newly wedded wife, and as she did so, she transformed completely from the imposing figure of divinity she had assumed for the coronation back to the laughing goddess I had first seen at Lancastyr Manor. "Queen Rose, the affliction of your father, Lord Lancastyr, is not a spell or a curse, but a malady of old age, a natural process with which it would be wrong for me to tamper. And it will worsen as the years pass. However, I can grant you the assurance that in the recesses of his mind lies his spirit—a spirit that will always love you."

I swallowed hard on the lump in my throat.

"Thank you, Ashiira," Rose said. I could tell it was the only thing she could manage to say without losing her composure.

Being human, it seemed, could sometimes mean feeling sorrow in the midst of ecstasy. I had much to learn in the years ahead, and my love would help me do it.

"There is one more gift I can give," Ashiira said. "King Charming and Queen Rose, you need not take up your responsibilities without a loving bulwark against your cares. For behold Lady Apricot and her attendants, whom I have brought from afar to live in the castle with you. They will share your joys and tribulations in the years to come."

My heart leapt. I caught sight of a tall, dignified female figure with an elegant sweep of pure white hair and a silver gown, who seemed to have appeared from nowhere but was making stately progress across the ballroom, flanked by two women of grace and gravity.

"Rose!" I cried. "Come meet my mother!"

I ran forward and embraced Lady Apricot, then held her at arm's length, surveying the pleasing aspect of her human shape. There was no reservation or doubt in my mother's expression; it was close to rapture. She did the human thing, kissing me on both cheeks as if she had done so many times before. Her scent was the sweet mother-scent I had always known, tinged with comforting apricot.

A king does not shed tears in public. I stepped back.

"You chose this path?" I demanded of her. "You wish to remain here with me, er, as you are? And Lady Lambchop and Lady Pudding, too?"

"We chose this fate together." She gave a regal dip of her head. Then her voice dropped to a whisper. "And just as your Cinderella named you Charming instead of Char, I'm afraid you must call my hand-maidens Lady Lila and Lady Petra from now on. The goddess said the Anglanders wouldn't understand otherwise."

I could not get over it. She was as sleek a human as she had been a rat. And she had given up everything she'd ever known to take on this new adventure with me.

"Did you think I would pass up the experience of someday holding my grandbabies?" she said, smiling. "Besides, my son, these humans turned out to be much, much smarter than I thought they were. They know how to appreciate quality when they see it. My son, king of Angland! Well, I can't say I'm surprised."

First, I presented her to my queen. They were rather formal together, though I could tell Rose was thrilled at this new development. *They have a long, long time to get to know each other,* I thought.

I then brought my mother forward and introduced her to our new family and friends, including Tumtry (who was quite taken with her, so much so that he seemed to perk up amazingly) and his proud, smiling ministers. I watched as Lady Apricot promised little Jessamyn a lapdog and plenty of bread and honey—and the same for her sister, Eustacia (when we could manage to find her). This pleased Jessamyn beyond reckoning.

And then the moment came when my mother met Rose's father. She put a hand to his bewildered face.

"See here, Barnaby de Lancastyr," she said in the bracing tone she had used with me when I was younger, "you have allowed everything to get into a most shocking state. I shall fix it, and help take care of you. Stay by my side."

"Very well, Apricot," Rose's father said. "I am already at your side. It is most comfortable here."

With this, Rose gave a cry of joy and flung her arms about my mother. Lady Apricot patted her head and made cooing noises.

Our happiness was now complete, and Ashiira clearly knew it.

In her own whimsical fashion, the goddess did not make a great spectacle of leaving us. In one moment the whole assembly was basking in each other's goodwill, as the awed spectators commenced to talk among themselves of the many omens and wonders they had just seen; and in the next, a tingling melody danced through the air. Ashiira's form had dissolved into a radiant whirlpool of gossamer light. It whirled round and round, growing smaller and brighter, approaching my queen, who faced it without a flinch.

I could tell Rose heard something in the shimmering wind that no one else could. There was a listening look on her face as she brought up her right hand to touch the glimmering sparks.

The music trickled to a stop. The azure light winked out.

And upon the third finger of my love's outstretched hand glowed a ring of rose gold, topped with a sapphire signet.

Epilogue

It is now many years later. The kingdom of Angland is prosperous and at peace. But our story is not over, though my dear queen and I are almost finished telling it.

I warned you from the very beginning: the Cinderella tale everyone seems to have heard is incorrect in almost every particular. Yet perhaps, after learning the truth in these pages, you can understand why she and I have been content to keep it that way until now.

Some of you, my dear readers, are our very own children and grandchildren. You—our beloved descendants—should be aware that your heritage is as strong and noble as it is unusual. If it is your fate to someday pass the test and rule Angland, be sure to bring to the throne not only human qualities, but rat ones as well.

Govern with heart—and know when to use your teeth.

Now the moment has come for me to admit that the highly popular version of Cinderella's tale did at least get one thing exactly right: how the story ended.

Oh.

My queen says she wishes to write the ending herself, so I shall hand over the quill to her, one last time:

— Happily Ever After —

Acknowledgments

*The lovely Mae Genovese.

*Sloane Matthews, for her sage advice.

*Insightful, generous Maria Bluni,
whose faith never wavered.

*My talented, caring author sisters of the WNP.

*Eric Myers and Margaret Ferguson—
extraordinary professionals, extraordinary people.

*My wonderful former colleagues and students
at the Marblehead Public Schools.

*Friends and family who have helped along the way.
Their names are written across my heart.

*Frances Hodgson Burnett, for the inspirational character
Melchisedec in A Little Princess.